Sapphire Stream

GARETH JACKSON

Cover design by: Victoria Emma

ISBN-13: 9798664154344

Winds Will Whisper

Part One

Sapphire Stream

Those who existed shall not be forgotten,

even though their feats were unwritten.

The winds will whisper of tales from our past,

and reveal the secrets once hidden…

Chapter One

A story, a great story, always starts fairly unremarkably. Either, '*Once upon a time*,' or, '*It has long been foretold*,' or something else sounding rather cliché. Because the beginning of a story is usually the hardest part. Where do you begin? The most exciting story can often fail with a typical, or unremarkable opening. So, there lies the question;

1

how do you begin what you believe to be a truly enchanting tale? One that will tantalise your senses, and immerse you into an unknown world beyond all recognition of that which you know to be true, to be real. And reel you so far in that you may never wish to come out. I suppose there is no right answer to that question, as everyone's preference of a great story is different. Has there ever been an opening so immaculately brilliant, that all stories should begin in such a way, or is it up to the reader, or listener, not to judge and take the journey anyway? The truth is, it is a question I do not know the answer to and probably never will. Therefore, I will not begin this story in the conventional way, and will leave you with another tale, told by another, and begin thereafter.

***

Her name is Solis, not because this means sun; although interestingly, like the sun being the oldest star in the universe, she too is the oldest member of her tribe; though no one knows quite how old. And she told the same tale, in exactly the same way, at exactly the same time of every single year. Although it is told to the children of Athia before they reach the age of five by their parents, and although their parents may tell the tale well, like Chinese whispers a story can alter. What makes the telling of the tale so special by

Solis, is that it is told to each child of Athia when they reach the age of five, before they receive their companion.

Each of the ten children, that reached the age of five before the Athianne celebrations marking the end of their year, were sat eagerly anticipating the story to be told. Or, at least as eagerly as any five-year-old can reasonably be expected to stay still. Parents were not present at this time, and children were left to walk into the ceremonial tent alone. Pinching, prodding and poking took place for ten minutes or so, before Solis made her grand entrance to the largest tent of the modest sized village.

The scent of her self-made perfume captured the attention of each of the children, like bumblebees to a fresh spring flower. Her movements were slow and graceful, yet the frailty of each step she made was well hidden under the enormity of her garments; which were also self-made, as most of the clothing was amongst the tribe. She wore a brightly coloured crown of feathers: dynamic reds, dazzling greens and deep blues. Her hair was chestnut brown, which was soft and settled by her shoulders. The Athianne were extraordinarily fortunate, in that from the day they are born until their time of passing, their hair remains unaltered, untainted by the trials of life. Her skin, however, was another story. She smiled an elderly smile, a trusting smile.

Like the children's favourite teacher in a classroom, they all sat in an orderly fashion in her presence. She too sat after they did. Her sheep's wool dress (which was also covered in brightly coloured feathers for decoration) trailed from her position on the floor, all the way back to where she had entered; and possibly a little further back toward her own tent, as it was immensely long.

The hungry eyes of the children rested upon the elderly Solis, as she rested her eyes upon the, now, well behaved younglings. She made sure each of them was paying attention.

Although you would not be able to see at a glance, as all the children were sat incredibly still, there was one among them who was sat even more so. One who did not partake in the childish antics before Solis arrived. It was probably due to the pressure such a child was placed under. Although only five years old, being the daughter of the chief was still a hefty burden to bear. Told from the day they could converse with their elders, that they are destined to rule, is not something that sits lightly upon a child's shoulders. Still, for little Soria, this did not seem to bother her one bit. Unaffected by the future that lay before her, it was not the weight of upcoming responsibility that had her pressed firmly into the floor with her legs crossed.

Some of the tribe thought her character was that of a child who was ignorant of her responsibility due to age, but others believed her character was due to evolution. Her ancestors had been the tribes leaders for centuries, so maybe their kin were born with natural leadership qualities. Perhaps the sweet innocence of infancy was all but wiped out from their gene pool, and they were ready to rule after learning to toddle. Either way, she struggled with friendships and never once showed any of the regular characteristics you would ordinarily have seen in a child.

Once Solis was convinced she had all the children's attention, she fixated her gaze on Soria. She gave her a short sharp smile, which was returned instantly and respectfully.

'Now children.' She began, then took a breath. 'We will begin your confirmation, as is the way of our tribe, with a tale. But, this is more than just a story. It is the story of our beginning and how the land we reside upon came to be. It is also out of respect to our guardian, who even now, watches over his land and makes sure we look after it. It is a wonderful tradition, which we carry out every year. It is because of this, and because we pay tribute to the guardian of the land, that he bestows upon us our companions. Let us begin with the story, by now you all know so well. Then, later, once you receive your companions, we can begin our annual celebrations.' She took another exaggerated breath and began…

'There once were two dragons that weren't very nice.
The red could breathe fire, and the white could breathe ice.

The valley they lived in was vast and wide,
and they each made their home on the opposite side.

The flaming hot dragon lived in a cavern,
on the highest peak of the tallest mountain.

The dragon with a white sparkly glow,
lived in a cave that was covered in snow.

The valley was wasteland, with no plants or trees,
It looked like a scene from nightmarish dreams.

Though desolate, dismal, and desperately dull,
they fought for the right to own it in full.

The dragon of ember had a raging hot temper,
and the white was as cold as a freezing December.

They clashed, crashed and clattered in showdowns of might,
locked in a tussle from day through to night.

They charged at high speed and lashed at each other,
the enormous echoes made the ground shake and shudder.

They both drew in breath, and puffed out their chests,
then they unleashed their power to see who was best.

The red dragon blew a boiling hot blaze,
that met with the white dragon's cold icy haze.

They both flapped their wings with fearsome force,
which caused winds that whirled without remorse.

They fought and they battled night after night,
they truly were equal on ground and in flight.
So, no one was going to win this fight.

The days went by, then weeks, months and years.
Until...
One day they stopped; for what had appeared?

The clash of these giants created a gully,
that ran down the middle of the nightmarish valley.

The flaming hot fire and the icy cold steam,
gave birth to a shimmering sapphire stream.

On either side of this sapphire stream,
grew plants, grass and trees, lush colours and green.

The wind from their wings blew seeds back and forth,
and in time forced a truly magnificent growth.

Their power was equal they both now agreed,
that their fighting was futile and fueled by greed.

There was no need to fight to test who was best,
both dragons bowed heads and flew back to their nests.

There now are two dragons, both kind and polite,
with no longer a need to meet up and fight.

They soar and they swoop, hover and glide,
admiring their valley as they fly side by side.'

The tent was alight with the flame of a flower known only in that part of the world. The Etherflame flowers burned a burnt orange flame, with flecks of reds and purples that it spat into the air. The flowers were placed in plant pots, to contain the fire to the plant only, as the fire of an Etherflame would only go out if starved of oxygen. Once the fire is put out, the flowers remain unharmed, ready to burn bright again; no one quite knows how this is possible.

They were neatly arranged around the outskirts of the interior of the tent. They expelled a pleasant scented white smoke which filled the room. The smoke was not harmful to the Athianne, as they were reared from the land of the red dragon. They could breathe in the fumes of a fire as though it was as fresh as the surrounding air. Their bodies were well adapted to a super-hot climate, and their skin, although soft as silk, was able to withstand a flame, if only for a short time before burning.

As the white smoke lingered above the heads of the children, it began to move with the words of Solis. The smoke moved to the rhythmic flow of her voice and began to enact the tale she spoke of. The younglings moved, thrilled, yet fearful of the re-enactment that played out before them. The sheer power of the two dragons at war, was less scary as a bedtime story, than it was to witness. All but

Soria were lifted from their bottoms and clambered to the sides of the tent, huddled together for safety. Soria was still sat solemnly in the centre of the room. Unaffected by the hubbub, she placed her arms out adoringly as the beasts floated passed her, stroking the smoke formations and watching them slip through her tiny fingers.

Solis, knowing the other children were in no more danger than they would be if they were tucked away in their beds, kept a watchful eye on Soria. The expression she donned was that of both curiosity and suspicion. Never before, not even a future leader of their tribe, had a child shown such unwavering bravery. Was it a good omen, or bad? It truly was difficult to determine. But Solis hid any doubt, however reasonable it may have been, behind the kindly smile of an elderly lady.

Once the story had finished, the tent curtain was opened, out went the smoke, swiftly followed by the rest of the children, who were now giggling and poking fun at each other for being scared of a little magic. Seeing the children out, and counting the heads as they did so, Solis stopped Soria at the exit.

She waited a minute and inspected her expression. She looked like she was about to speak, but Solis jumped in first with a question. 'Did you enjoy the story child?' she asked with a smile.

'Very much so Miss. It just seems a little short.' She said disappointedly.

Solis looked at her fascinated. 'Short, Child?'

'Yes, Miss. I would very much like to know a bit more about the white dragon, and the people that live on the opposite side of the Sapphire Stream. I thought, today, we might learn a little more about the others?'

'Oh, you are an inquisitive child aren't you.' She said flatteringly, then continued. 'But those are stories for another time. You are only five years old, yet you bear the head of someone twenty years your senior. You should not need to know anything other than what you already do, until the time is right. You still have lots of child left in you to let free before you become Chieftainess of Athia. After the end of today, you will have a companion. A fine, strong companion no doubt, like that of your parents, and their parents before them. But as a child, a companion is a best friend for fun. A bond must be formed through play and exploration. Then, when the time is right, and you are ready to take your place as our leader, you will be readied with the knowledge you seek. For now though child, focus on fun.'

It took a few seconds longer than expected, as though Soria was expecting a different, a further answer, perhaps a less defensive answer. But after a short while she smiled and responded, 'Yes, Miss.'

'Oh less of the, Miss, child. I have known more members of your family than years you have lived, and I have seen even more of them grow and pass than I care to count. Solis is fine as you well know.'

11

'Sorry, Solis.' She said respectfully.

Solis gave her a firm nudge between the shoulders 'Now be off with you child.' She said kindly, and Soria ran off swiftly to catch up with the rest of the group.

'I do wonder about that one.' She whispered rhetorically to herself as she saw her dart off into the distance. Then she returned to the tent to put out the brightly burning flowers.

***

At that exact same moment in time, the exact same thing was happening on the other side of the valley. The story, you see, was true; albeit watered down for the consumption of children. The dragons that occupied the valley long ago had fought ferociously over who would rule it all. And, those dragons had calmed themselves over time. The Sapphire Stream that is spoken of in the short rhyme does exist and it is the life source of all that reside in the valley on both sides. Even though the tale was over a thousand years old, the valley dwellers believed that the dragons still lived.

It is said that the breath of the sleeping dragon of fire is so hot, that it is the reason for the intense heat that fills the air of the Athianne side, the right-hand side of the stream. It is also the reason the right-hand side of the Sapphire Stream is so hot, that the steam which rises from it would singe the skin of even the Athianne.

However, on the opposite side, where the Glacianne tribe reside, the air is much colder. The dragon that sleeps on the other side, is said to breathe out snow as he snores. It is so cold in fact, that the gentle breeze above the stream on the left-hand side would freeze you instantly, should you dare try and venture across it. So, should anything happen to either one of the sleeping dragons, the stream would either boil due to the intense heat, or freeze over completely. Either way would disrupt the very fabric of life it supports.

It is for this reason, that the tribes devote their lives to preserving the land, and revering their guardian dragons. It has been a long time since both tribes have come into contact with one another. So long in fact, that the land itself was barren wasteland. A time before the dragons arrived.

When the white and red dragon arrived long ago, the tribes once fought against them as violently and tirelessly as they fought each other, believing them to be a source of pure evil. It was only when they saw what was happening to the land they lived in, that they chose to stand back and leave them be, to settle their quarrel alone. Once the great war of the beasts was over, those who were on the right-hand side gave thanks to the red dragon and worshipped him as a deity. The red dragon then bestowed upon them a gift of his own fire. An eternal flame which will never go out so long as the dragon lives; or so the story goes. But as with any story, there are many renditions.

Those who were left stranded on the left-hand side, were too offered a gift by the white dragon. Before it went into a deep hibernation, the dragon shed its skin and gave it to the Glacianne tribe as a kind gesture for their reverence of the beast. It is said that, so long as no harm befalls him, the skin will remain intact, otherwise it would crumble to the ground like powdered snow. The enormity of the white dragon's shed skin was enough to create a shelter for the Glacianne tribe. The scales still remain an impenetrable barrier from the harsh cold of the left-hand side of the Sapphire Stream. Although the Glacianne are now climatized, and walk freely amongst the frozen forestry, there was a time when the dragon's hide offered much needed protection from the frost; a home for all against the harsh cold.

There were eight Glacianne children turning five this festival season. Eight Glacianne children had been told the tale by an elder of their own tribe.

Oddly enough, the chief of the Glacianne tribe also had a daughter that had come of age. Born on exactly the same day, at exactly the same time as Soria. It could not be said why, nor would the people of the Athianne, or the Glacianne tribe have ever known it, but it marked significance.

Her name was Ohmiya. She was of a different nature altogether to Soria; a free spirit. She cared little of anything other than what she was doing at that moment in time and was always freefalling into

14

danger. Although sometimes troublesome, she was loved by all that came into contact with her and adored by all the tribes folk alike.

It was at the same time that Soria, and the younglings of the Athianne tribe, were being taken to receive their companions from their guardian, that the Glacianne younglings were being taken for theirs.

Chapter Two

'Keep up kiddies.' Said one of the elders of the Glacianne tribe, then she gazed over and counted the heads of the disorderly line behind her. 'Where is Ohmiya?' she grunted.

'Here I am!' Came a squeaky noise from through trees ahead of the group.

'You know you are not to venture off without us Ohmiya. You may be the chief's daughter, but you are not an exception to the rules. Especially not when we are venturing outside the safety of the village. These mountains can only be navigated by trained professionals. Children would likely get lost and freeze to death, eventually, without a tribe elder, or worse. We are not the only occupants of this land and you should respect the wildness of Glacia; for she may choose to take unwary miscreants if she so chooses.' The elder spoke as though speaking to a well-behaved teenager, if ever there was such a thing. Realising the child was unaware of the danger she was in, the tribe elder rubbed her roughly on the top of her whitened blonde hair and said softly, 'come on you. You'll be the death of me if your mother and father find out I lost you before we even reached the entrance of the great guardian's cave.'

'Sorry Freya.' Said Ohmiya in an innocent childlike manor.

Freya stood tall. She was one of the tallest Glacianne women at nearly seven feet. She was strong as an ox, yet as agile as a gazelle. Few Glacianne men could best her in combat and she was trusted absolutely by the chief. The trip to the entrance of the cave, where the guardian is supposed to slumber, was a treacherous journey. Few outsiders would have made it fully grown, yet by the age of five, Glacianne children were hardened enough to brave to fiercest frosty weathers.

Freya awaited Ohmiya's return to the flock, as she had yet again wandered off, and gave all the younglings a stern look. 'Let it be said to all of you. You will all, each of you, one day, be able to walk the land of Glacia with your companion for protection.' She stopped talking abruptly, as though she had still to finish what she was saying, then stroked the large white dire wolf that stood beside her. It stood half as tall as she did, its fur coat shone superbly in the light of the low sun. Its fur was coarse like that of a Glacianne's hair. Sharp as barbs, yet soft to stroke at the hands of its keeper. Its face was fierce, but it was completely harmless to any who did not pose a threat to Freya. Its loyalty was absolute, so long as its keepers was also. She turned back to the younglings after petting it firmly several times behind its large pointy ears. 'But, for now you must all follow me.'

A companion is so much more than a pet. Some may look like your average animal, but they possess unique qualities that you would not see in any other creature.

'Go up ahead boy.' Said Freya to her companion. 'You know what to do if you see any.'

Any what? Thought Ohmiya.

The wolf was fast. So fast in fact, that it was barely visible to anyone but Freya. It jumped onto a nearby branch that had broken from its tree. Then jumped from that branch to another, and so on and so forth. Until, all you could hear was the whistling of the wind that was blowing between its crystallised fur coat. Freya's focus never left the road ahead, but her companion saw all from high above.

The group walked on for a short while. Suddenly, the whistling sound stopped. Freya raised her right arm sternly, which forced all the younglings to a grinding halt, although some continued on and crashed into the other in front.

'Shh!' she said to the loudly whispering younglings.

All went quiet. All but a loud thudding noise that came from a short distance up ahead. Then a loud, but low toned, howl captured the attention of Freya. She never spoke, but her gestures said a thousand words. Everyone was pushed to one side behind a large fern tree. Freya grabbed a large dangling branch and wrapped it around everyone like a great green shield. The branch of a Glacianne fern was as strong as steel, yet her expression was not strained as she pulled it back. She gestured again for all to be quiet and not one of the younglings would have contested.

The thudding noise came closer, and closer, and closer, until it stopped. Then one large white foot hit the ground before them with a wallop. Every child was lifted from their feet for a second and hit the powdered snow with their behinds. Too frightened to move, though, everyone remained seated in the wet snow; all but Ohmiya, who was too inquisitive by nature to not want to see what was attached to the great white foot behind the green fern.

What is it, she thought, as she peered through the gaps in the trees. Whatever was attached to the foot was too tall to see. She tried to take a step closer, but was sharply pulled back by the free hand of Freya.

Everyone stayed dead still until the, whatever it was, moved on. A huge gust of grotty smelling mist fell from the sky. It was hard for the younglings to hold back the vomit that was about to pour from their tiny mouths. The bad breath of the beast lingered on the air, even after it had left. As it walked away, they could hear its clumsy walk and its claws accidently catch the fern trees' trunk.

It was several minutes later that Freya finally let go of the branch which whipped out with a twang.

'What was that?' asked Ohmiya excitedly.

Freya looked a foot or so shorter than usual, because she was stood within the large oval footprint. She bent low and sniffed the surface of the floor like a blood hound, then stood up again and winced. She did not answer Ohmiya's question. Instead she stepped out of the footprint in the ground and made her way back to the large fern. She stretched out her arm as high as she could reach and stroked her hand across one of the two slash marks in the tough tree trunk.

'What was that thing?' Ohmiya was unrelenting with her questions.

Freya's companion fell from the trees gracefully and landed by her side. Its feet made little impression in the snow and its landing made little impression on anyone's ears.

'Good boy.' She said. 'If it wasn't for you we would all be yeti chowder.'

'So it was a yeti. That's so cool. I've always wanted to see one.'

Freya turned abruptly and stamped her foot firmly in the ground, which forced Ohmiya to tumble backward. 'Damn it child!' she pointed jaggedly at Ohmiya. 'You will be the death of us all if you do not learn to do as you are told! I like you. I do. And our guardian knows I would do anything for you. But one more foot out of line and I will feed you to the forest myself. Do you not realise how much danger we were just in?'

Freya had never looked so cross. Ohmiya knew that she tested the boundaries of acceptable behaviour, but never before had she made anyone lose it.

'I'm... I'm... I'm sorry!' Ohmiya's eyes had begun to well up with tears.

Freya looked at Ohmiya, like a mother unable to stay mad at her child. 'No, I'm sorry. I forget your age. Of course you wish to understand the world around you better and all that resides within it. It's just that, this mountain scape is not the place for lessons on Glacia. Those are better kept for later, at home, when we are all once again safe.'

'If it is so dangerous, why does the guardian not just send our companions down to where we live? Why do we have to walk all the way up to the top? If our companions keep us safe on the way up, why make us walk up without them first?' she asked in a manor beyond her years.

Freya looked at her with adoration. She had forgotten just how bright young Ohmiya was. Yes, she was free spirited and it was testing to imagine her as a leader. But, every now and again, she could see how truly astounding she was.

'You are a perceptive little one.' She bent low and offered her a hand up. 'Long before we became civilised, our people would send their children up the mountain alone. Only the strongest and bravest would return with a companion from the guardian. It was a test, you see; a rite of passage. The festivities at the end would then be a celebration for those who had returned, and a memorial of those who had not. And, it is not the very top we go, it is only the first of three entrances to cave. The very top is where the guardian sleeps. Only with wings could one hope to reach the top from outside. Otherwise it is a perilous, most likely suicidal scale of Glacia's mountain scape. But, then again, no one truly knows, as no one has ever tried to get to the topmost entrance. It may not be as treacherous, if one were to simply walk through the cave entrance and follow the paths through it. But, it is out of both respect and fear, that no one and nothing has ever entered.'

Ohmiya looked a little startled at this enlightenment and Freya quickly changed her tone to a chirpier one.

'But this tradition has long since evolved into a more acceptable festival. No longer are children sent to their slaughter and are now guided, usually gently, up the mountain by a well-trained Glacianne and returned safely home for a huge party.'

Ohmiya, still a little shaken by her words, raised a light smile.

'But, I seriously doubt anything would ever happen to you; even alone.'

'Why?' asked Ohmiya.

'Because of your ancestral line.'

'What do you mean?'

'Because.' She whispered softly in Ohmiya's ear. 'Your great, great, great - and probably a few great's thereafter - grandfather, was the last to return from the mountain on a lone venture. And it was his strength and resilience against the extremes of Glacia at that time, that made the people choose him as leader of the people. Since then, it has been your family that has led our tribe into the glorious civilization that we have come to be today.'

The proudness in Ohmiya's face was not well hidden, as she beamed with delight at this.

'And I am sure, when you come of age, that you will rule with the same might, and grace, that all of your family has done before you.' She paused then continued jokingly 'But for now, could you try not to kill us all by the hands of a hungry snowman?'

They both laughed and they continued on their way.

***

The Athianne children, although still childish by nature, were less childlike than their distant relations on the other side of the Sapphire Stream. They played when out of the presence of parents, yet they behaved all too well before most grownups. They were also headed to toward the mountainous peaks of Athia, but in a slightly more orderly fashion.

The blazing heat of Athia beat down hard on the heads of the tiny travellers. The humidity was so intense that it was like breathing in liquid. The Etherflame flowers that grew wildly were ablaze from the heat. They grew separate from the other plants, and although plants cannot see, hear or think for themselves, it is believed that they grow apart from the rest of the plant life to avoid wildfire. The land's plants, trees and creatures were climatized enough to withstand heat and flame for a time, but the Etherflame's fire was unlike any other, and even those most hardened would eventually succumb to it.

Unlike the huge green ferns, and the monsters that lived within the Glacianne forest, Athia is more open. There were more plants and flowers than trees. It wasn't quite desert like, but vegetation grew shorter, softer and more colourful. Yet the whole land is tainted with a blood orange glow. The creatures are less vicious, less scary, and less likely to attack the Athianne. They may have been a muscly warrior race, but their diet was shared with *most* of the creatures, and they all took an equal share of the lands resources. Neither the Athianne, nor the creatures took more than their fill, and neither one was in competition with the other. Less available natural resources in Glacia had forced a more carnivorous diet, by both Glacianne and creature alike, which proved for a more hostile arrangement.

But unlike the creatures that could crunch on the bones of unsuspecting younglings in Glacia, Athianne were less worried about the wildlife, and more concerned with the length of the journey. At that moment in time, the Glacianne younglings had a far more perilous trip, but they were almost at their destination. The Athianne, however, had a much farther trip to reach the first of the three mountain peaks of Athia. The peaks were tall and sharp like knives when looked at from a distance. At the foot of the first knife edged peak, it looked almost like a vertical climb. No one had ever ventured higher than that of the first peak, and aside from their guardian, no one truly knew what resides upon the other two.

Stood a little in front of Soria was Argon. He, like Freya, was one of the tribes foremost trusted elders. He had long silken black hair, like all Athianne had, darkened skin with a caramel tinge, like all Athianne had, and an inviting, trustworthy face, which most Athianne did not have. In fact, the only two that looked remotely friendly were Solis and Argon. All the others had a face of thunder.

He halted brashly at the foot of the first peak and turned to face the younglings. 'Right, you lot!' he discharged a loud booming voice from the pit of his stomach with a straight face, and without ever looking as though he was shouting.

Soria stopped instantly, as though she had anticipated the instruction. The others stopped in an orderly fashion, close together, yet a few paces behind Soria. She took a stern look behind her at the child directly to her rear. The child looked a little worried and took a further step back, forcing the others to do so. It may not have been her intent, but even at only five, she had the look of a leader.

'Now, we climb!' he boomed again.

Soria nodded in confirmation, and the rest of the younglings stooped their heads when Argon turned to face the rock's face. When he turned back they all stood back up resolute and proceeded to climb. Soria was already part of the way up before the others had made a start. It may have looked vertical from afar, but being on all fours was not necessary and one could have quite easily walked, if the effort was put in.

Argon waited for the last of them to start climbing before making his way up behind them. It was customary for the children to begin this journey on their own without direct supervision - even though he was directly behind them - to mark the start of their journey in life without aid. Only a hundred years or so before, were children left at the bottom of the mountain to make the journey alone. And like the

Glacianne, their ritual was pretty much the same. Those who perished were mourned, and those who made it back prevailed as honorary Athianne.

***

The Glacianne younglings and Freya had made it to the cave entrance that was located to the east of Glacia, and east of the Sapphire Stream. There was a soft wind that had followed them up the snowy mountain, which stopped as they reached the cave entrance. They all stood in an awkward fashion, like a huddle, behind Freya. She moved away from them and onto a snowy surface. It was the first opening they had come across since the start of their journey; no trees just a flat blanket of snow. Beyond the flat plain of whiteness, was a pitch-black opening. It looked like a never-ending pool of darkness, and should one venture in, one might never return to see the light of day.

'Come forth Ohmiya. As the chief's daughter, and next in line as leader of our tribe, you shall be the first to claim your companion from our guardian.' She said proudly.

Ohmiya hesitated, and for the first time to be witnessed by anyone, she seemed nervous.

'No.' She responded, with more to come. 'I wish for the others to receive theirs first. I am not more important than anyone else. So, if anything, I should be last. My father told me; you can't assume as leader, that your life is more important than anyone else's. Without anyone to lead, there is no reason for a leader. A leader who believes they are more important than those who they lead, has already failed.'

She memorised her father's words perfectly, and although partially true, she did not fully understand their meaning. It was more fear of the cave entrance, and fear of her future companion that compelled her to sound so virtuous. *I could not hope to tame a huge dire wolf such as Freya's,* she quietly thought to herself, amongst other anxieties.

Freya, unaware of Ohmiya's true fears, almost welled up with pride at her future leader. This pride forced a curtsy from Freya. 'Very well. Come forth Cienna. You shall be the first to receive your companion. The rest of you form a more orderly line and come up one at a time.'

Cienna was trembling at the knees as she walked up to the entrance. It was a great honour to be picked first, as it was usually the chief's child who would be first to receive their companion. Never in modern times, had an ordinary tribe folk's child gone first. Not only that, children are not given any description whatsoever as to what happens when they reach the cave entrance. They do not know if they are tasked with anything, or if they have any other challenge to overcome.

'Stand right there.' Said Freya softly, then pointed to a patch of unspoiled white snow on the floor and stepped back to the others.

The other younglings, Ohmiya included, looked nervous and made low worried noises. Freya stood still and smiled as she watched Cienna in the centre of the powdered snow platform. The soft wind stopped and sound evacuated the area. All was quiet except for the clattering of Cienna's knees. She looked up at the cave entrance and to either side of the opening. Etched into the grey rocky surface was the image of a dragon, on both sides. It was presumably what the white dragon was supposed to look like. Each of the carved-out dragons stared at her, like the eyes of a painting that seem to move continuously in your direction. All was quiet for a few moments. Then a light began to emerge from the cave's entrance. It was a dazzling sparkly light, which looked as though glitter had been thrown into the path of a torch light.

The light hovered for a few seconds more, until a low-pitched cawing came from within. It grew louder and louder still, until an explosion of light came from the entrance, like a party popper, and landed over Cienna. It was blinding, terrifying. Had she received her companion, or had she been gobbled up by a giant monstrous eagle?

The light faded and a laughing sound came from Cienna. She was giggling and a cooing noise was also apparent. The light completely vanished and, there on her left shoulder, was the most adorable owl you ever did see. It was not your typical owl, as no companion was completely animal, and all possessed magical properties. It was only a baby, as all companions begin life, not as a new-born, but as young as their keepers. It was glitter white with a coarse feathery sheath, and had big black pearl-like eyes. It splayed each wing which split in two; four wings which flapped like two. It was burrowing its forehead lovingly into Cienna's neck, which was making her chuckle hysterically. An instant bond was formed and she made her way back to the rest of the group with her new companion.

The rest of the children, now seemingly unafraid, readied themselves to receive their very own companion. They all sprinted gleefully into the centre staging area and awaited the light to bestow upon them a magical creature to play with.

One by one they returned: A fox, a bear, a seal, a squirrel, a hare and lastly another fox, which seemed to be the prevailing creature, all with coarse glitter white coats, all with remarkably unique features and no doubt abilities.

Ohmiya was still hesitant. *What would I receive?* She continued to think. Her doubt was alien to her. Never had she had a doubt in her mind about anything. It was like she was subconsciously waiting for something before she could move out to receive her companion. *What* was she waiting for?

Freya gave her a soft nudge between the shoulders and pushed her forward. 'Go on.' She said eagerly. 'You've waited long enough. Go receive your companion.'

She walked slowly up to the centre of the powder snow opening before the cave entrance. So slow in fact, it was as though her speed was being dictated by an unknown force. As though she could not receive her companion just yet. The timing was not quite right. Until, it was. She felt a sudden urge to move quicker. The fear had subsided and she was once again excited at the prospect of receiving her companion.

She stood still awaiting the light to re-emerge.

***

In Athia, Soria had made it to the top of the first peak, ten minutes or so quicker than the rest of the group. She stomped her feet and paced impatiently on the red, dusty surface. She, too, felt compelled to move at an eerie speed, a much faster pace than usual, and reach the peak first. She could often be impatient, and wish for things to occur far faster than they did; *it will be quicker to do it myself,* was her usual attitude, which was unlike the usual attitude of a youngling. But, at that moment, she felt a great urge to reach the peak at a specific time, as though fate willed it so.

The rest of the younglings were far too far behind for her to wait any longer. She ran to the cavern entrance with intent and stood in the centre platform, which was a charcoal black colour and not at all covered in snow like Glacia's cave entrance. There was not an archway entrance to the cavern either. It was acutely triangle and the mountain peak was a darkened brown colour with flecks of black soot. It too had dragons etched into either side of the entrance, and they too had their eyes firmly fixated on Soria.

She did not stand still. She was moving on the spot like she was in need of relieving herself and looking for a nearby toilet. 'Come on.' She spouted in a loud whisper. 'Where is it?' she whispered ever so slightly louder.

The entrance to the cavern had begun to swirl, like the infinitely dark entrance had become a whirlpool. The black whirlpool at the entrance began to alter state. It began to change to a deep orange, then red, then a mixture of molten colours. Soria was not remotely scared. She became as excited as a kid in a candy store. What would have struck fear into the heart of most, had her overwhelmed with joy. This was it. She was about to receive her companion. *I hope it's strong, I hope it's powerful, I hope it's the only one of its kind.* She thought to herself as she rubbed her hands together.

Then something appeared from within the entrance. Something unexpected approached her. Something, that no one could have predicted as the companion of the future leader of the Athianne tribe.

'What are you?' she asked unimpressed. 'Is this a joke?'

***

At that exact same moment, at the exact same time, something else appeared before the cave entrance in Glacia. Something unexpected approached Ohmiya. Something that was probably a fitting companion for such a character. Something that probably wasn't what you would describe as a leader's companion. But something that was most suited to a child like Ohmiya. Everyone else looked a little stunned, as they awaited her to say something; to do something.

'Oh wow! It's so cute! I love it!' she shouted with delight.

Chapter Three

F reya held back the other younglings and ordered her wolf to keep them all steady. She was curiously fearful of the creature that had emerged from the cave. It was not like any companion she had come across before. It had neither the characteristics that could link it to any known animal, nor the characteristics that could link it to any creature of myth. It had been known, albeit very rare, that a child should receive a peculiar beast from their guardian; a lizard that looked almost dragon like, and an ape that could have passed as part yeti. But, none like the one that stood before Ohmiya.

It was short and stumpy, with large oval eyes that covered a third of its body. They were a deep blue and were staring directly into the eyes of Ohmiya. It looked rather small and unthreatening; the shape of a semi-circle with a spiny, sparkly white fur coat, as though a white coconut had been cut in half and planted in the snow. It had no visible knees and two tiny feet which poked out from under it.

It didn't move. Neither did Ohmiya. They just stared intently at each other. Freya edged closer towards the pair with caution. Ohmiya held her arms out and called it over like a stray dog. 'Come on.' She insisted. 'Don't be frightened.'

Freya was concerned and whispered at her to wait. But Ohmiya was too excited to listen and kept beckoning the creature over. 'Don't be scared, I won't hurt you, I promise.'

The little thing began to waddle in her direction at a pace no faster than that of snail. 'Wait.' Freya whispered a little louder. 'Wait right there.' She said as she tried to make up ground a little quicker and make her way between Ohmiya and her new companion.

The creature saw Freya moving closer and began to act nervous, although it was hard to tell, as it wore no expression. It stopped and Ohmiya went to meet it the rest of the way. Freya tried to intervene beforehand, but it was too late. 'Be careful.' She said.

Ohmiya lifted it in the air like a new puppy, let out a loud shriek and fell over into the snow. Freya sprinted the rest of the way to her. Then she stopped. She was not screaming in fear, nor was she in any pain. She was howling hysterically as her new companion rubbed its bristly coat against her hands and then her face.

Freya stood over them and looked down. 'You're playing?' she said to herself rhetorically.

'What is it?' asked Ohmiya through her laughter.

'I have no idea.' Responded Freya. 'No idea whatsoever. Just be careful with that thing. It could bite, or...'

'...Or what? How can it bite?' replied Ohmiya, then turned the fuzzy coconut with feet towards her. 'It has no teeth.'

Ohmiya's new companion smiled a wide toothless grin at Freya. 'So it doesn't. Still, just be careful with it, until we get back. Maybe one of the other elders in the tribe knows what it is.'

'How come you don't know what it is?' Ohmiya asked as she snuggled with her companion in the powdered snow.

Freya scratched her head, puzzled by the creature. 'Honestly? I've never seen anything like it.' Even though it seemed harmless, and harmless it certainly did look, Freya was fearful of the unknown. A natural born hunter, she seemed constantly on her guard; even during the festivities, she would stand on the outskirts of the main ceremonies and remain ever watchful of her surroundings.

'So, I am the only one with a companion like it? You hear that Snowflake? You're unique.'

Freya raised an eyebrow. 'Snowflake? You named it already?'

'Of course he has a name. It was either that, or Mr. Fuzzy.' She said whilst rubbing its bristly fur against her cheek.

'I think that Snowflake is a great choice.' *If they were the only two choices,* she thought to herself.

Freya called over her companion with a whistle. The wolf lifted Ohmiya from the ground by the hood of her coat, like it would a cub, and brought her back to the rest of the younglings.

'Look what I got.' Ohmiya said to the rest of them with extreme enthusiasm.

The rest of the younglings looked unsure how to respond. It truly was an odd-looking thing. There was very little of it to compliment, as there was very little of it at all. No wings, no strong (or even visible) limbs, no facial expression (for the most part anyway). Just two oversized blue eyes punched into the middle of a fury white semi-circle, and penguin like feet. 'Cute, huh?' she sought out some response from her young peers.

Cienna was the first to offer a complement. She felt highly guilty of taking the first spot. Whilst stroking her snowy white owl under the chin, she believed herself to have robbed her future leader of a worthy companion.

The rest of the younglings then spoke up, 'Very cute.' They all agreed and gave a nod.

'I know, right? Isn't he, though?' Ohmiya gave Snowflake a big squeeze, then looked at Freya for instruction.

Still a little confused, it was a few seconds before she realised she had the attention of the younglings. Unusually quiet and awaiting what to do next, they stared at Freya.

'Right, ah, yes!' she spoke louder with every word then cleared her throat. 'Now everyone has a companion, we shall make our way back down the mountain. No more than a few hours hike down I should say. It's far quicker going down than coming up. However, we will still need to be vigilant.' She turned to Ohmiya. 'Which means no running off and no wondering away from the group. Your companions are a long way off being able to protect you from, or forewarn you of any immediate threat.' Again, she turned to look at the small white fuzzball in Ohmiya's loving embrace. 'A long way off. So all of you need to follow me closely and we will make it back to the village in good time. Just before the festivities begin.'

***

The last of the Athianne younglings had her arms clung tight around Argon's neck. He reached the top shortly after the others, who were stood still a little distance from Soria. He made his way through the crowd and lowered the littlest of the younglings, Aylen, carefully to the floor. Exhaustion was expected of a few. It was a rare case indeed, if ever it was to have happened, that all the younglings would make it to the top first try. It had been known that none at all would make it, which was the main reason that the Athianne altered their ways. No longer were parents willing to send their children to their death.

The Athianne tribe was all but depleted in numbers, before the elders decided to lead them up to the first mountain peak. It took many years, but the tribes numbers gradually rose again over time, until they could no longer be deemed an endangered race.

Argon gazed over at Soria, who was stood with her back facing him. 'Is this a joke?' she snarled.

Argon walked up behind her and placed his hand on her shoulder. 'You should have slowed down Soria. We need to all be together before we begin.'

Soria never turned to look at him, as her gaze was still fixated dead ahead.

'What are you looking at?' he rose his head and looked over at the odd-looking thing that stared directly at Soria like a lost pet. With his free hand, he quickly put two fingers to his mouth, pursed his lips and whistled sharply. A deafening screech fell from above, and bolt of red and blue dove from the sky. A falcon, that looked part phoenix landed his arm. It gripped his arm tightly with its talons, which looked sharp enough to slice through bone, yet left no visible marks on its keeper. The squawking echoed throughout the mountains like a battle cry and sent a chill down the spine of all the younglings nearby. 'Easy girl!' he patted and stroked the bird affectionately on its neck, which calmed it down.

'What is it? Where did it come from?' he asked.

Soria was quiet for a second before she eventually replied. 'I don't know.' She said bleakly. 'It just came out from the opening in the mountain, there...' she pointed, 'between the two dragons.'

'It couldn't have.' He said puzzled. 'The only things that come out of the cave are the companions our guardian bestows upon us.' He scratched under his chin, looked deep in thought and let out a sigh. 'This creature doesn't look like any companion I have ever seen before. Let alone one I would expect to be fitting for you.'

Soria, still focused on the creature before her, suddenly turned to the rest of the younglings. 'It must be a mistake then. The guardian must have given me the wrong companion. It must be for you.' She pointed rudely at Aylen.

The other younglings looked lost for words, as their future ruler held her finger up angrily in their direction.

Argon lowered her finger gently. 'Our guardian does not make mistakes little one.' She looked up at him worried. 'If it truly came out of the cave entrance, the way you said it did, then this companion is yours, no other's.'

She turned again to the cavern entrance where it stood. Like Ohmiya's companion, the resemblance was uncanny. It was the same shape, albeit a vibrant red colour with flecks of orange embedded in its fur, which could have easily been mistaken for a naked flame. Its fur was soft like that of the Athianne tribes hair. Its eyes were like shiny black pebbles, that made up a third of its tiny body. With no visible limbs, it also waddled like a penguin; and it had begun to waddle toward her.

As she made her way towards it, it began to smile a toothless grin, a loving grin. Soria stared sternly at it, with no sign of affection in her face. It brushed its fuzzy fur against her bare leg affectionately and made cooing noises. *This has got to be a joke,* she pondered, looking at the creature unimpressed and finding it hard to return a smile.

'Are you kidding me!' she bellowed, which echoed up the mountain range. Then kicked the little thing away from her leg and walked back towards the others.

'You must not disrespect our guardian Soria. Your companion is for life. You receive no other, and no other will protect you and look out for you the way your companion will.'

She pointed rudely at the creature. 'This thing cannot protect me. I can protect myself better. I wanted a fearless beast, not a fuzzy pet.'

'You may be disappointed, but you do not know what this creature will grow to be. My companion started out life looking like a multicoloured sparrow. Now look at her.' He gestured to the great bird, and how big she was, that perched on his forearm. 'Maybe, your companion will become more impressive than you could ever imagine. Maybe it is the strongest companion ever to have existed. After all, a human baby is the least impressive being on the planet. Insects start out life more able than that of a new-born. Your companion may just be slow to grow into itself. Give it time. Nurture it, train it, be its friend. By the time you are old enough to lead, this little guy could grow to be truly magnificent.'

Argon had a trusting, wise face, and so it was hard to dismiss his words as untruthful. Although he himself was unsure if what he was saying was true.

He hurried the rest of them to the edge of the charcoal black circle platform. 'Off you go Aylen, you go next.'

Aylen was nervous, more so because of the scornful scowls aimed at her from Soria, than of receiving her companion. She walked cautiously toward the cavern's entrance, which was impossibly black and uninviting. A slight tremble in her hand turned to a shake, so she grabbed it with the other. She turned back to Argon and he ushered her along with his hand gestures, so she continued on.

Unsure of what to do when she reached the cavern's entrance, she just remained dead still. A light gust whizzed behind her, which made her jump a little. Then, the entrance began to swirl again. It burned bright like the fires of hell and looked as though it could suck you in at any point. But, it did not suck her in. Instead, it spat something out.

A baby red wolf sprang from the entrance and landed on its feet in front of Aylen. It was large for a new companion. So large in fact, it looked halfway to being fully grown. Its fur mimicked the sun, as solar flares erupted on the surface of its coat.

Aylen fell back and tried to scurry away on her bottom. The wolf caught up to her in a flash. She stopped and shielded her face with her hand. Then, she laughed. A bristly wet tongue pressed up against her palm. She lifted up her hand to see the smiling, panting wolf stood in front of her. It gave her cheek the same treatment as her hand, until she was coated in a crystal-clear drool. Aylen wrapped her arms around its neck and it pulled her to her feet. Standing at her height, it was an impressive size indeed for a new-born companion.

Argon and the rest of the younglings clapped, as the pair made it back to the group. Soria was unimpressed and crossed her arms crossly. She refused to even look at Aylen, and gave a scornful stare at her own companion that was glued to her leg. She gave it a swift kick with her foot to knock it away, but it returned faithfully and stuck back to her leg. *You better grow to be even better than Aylen's wolf,* she thought to herself.

'Right, next, come on everyone, let's keep this line moving, we're burning daylight.' Said Argon. The rest of the younglings were far less fearful than Aylen to approach the entrance. Aylen was oddly reserved for an Athianne child. She was, as all Athianne younglings were, well-behaved and polite. But she was not as fearless as the rest. She would follow the instruction of an elder without question, but that did not mean she was happy about everything that was asked of her. The other Athianne children were less in tune with the idea of consequence. They trusted the voice of an elder and would readily jump off a cliff if it was asked of them.

One by one, they stood before the cavern entrance, and one by one, they received their companions: a bear, a bird of some kind, a deer, another deer, another bird, a large cat, a dog and another cat. Like that of the Glacianne companions, they were not simply animals. The companions of the Athianne younglings were, indeed as extraordinary as those that had just been given on the opposite side of the Sapphire Stream.

However, as both sets of younglings made their way back to the villages they came from, one thing was apparent, something very strange had occurred during that year's ritual.

Chapter Four

T he Glacianne younglings, led by Freya, had arrived back home. The gates that formed the entrance to the Glacianne tribe's village, were large cut down fern trees, and the edges had been sharpened into pikes. Some had been speared vertically into the ground to form a solid barrier, and others had been forced in at an angle, with the sharp end facing outward to deter outsiders and hungry beasts from trying to enter. The blistering cold had given the pikes a glittery, ice white shine.

The heavily fortified barrier was not a regular shape, as it had been formed around the shed skin of the guardian dragon. Watch posts were positioned every hundred metres.

The tired travellers wandered through the greenery and out in to the open. Covered from head to toe in a powdered snow, they were unseen by those who were on duty. Freya came out from the trees last, and drew a small horn immediately from under her animal skin coat. It was carved from the tip of a mammoth tusk, that had been caught earlier that year for food.

Glacianne hunters would once produce a high-pitched whistle to signal the opening of the gates, should the watchtowers not spot their arrival. However, it was an unfortunate event which had occurred only a few years prior, that led them to change their approach. The creatures of Glacia had become smarter and more cunning. A wolf pack, known only to Glacia, picked up on the signal. They were somehow able to mimic the whistling noise, and unwary guards opened the gates. Since then, they have alternated the signal at random, so no mistakes could be made as to whom was awaiting entry.

The loud noise that came from the horn was as deep as thunder. It echoed through the land like a Viking war horn, and ventured further than the land of Glacia, I dare say.

The gates had begun to open immediately. They did not fling open like that of a draw bridge, though, as the mechanism was hand powered. Large wheels carved from ancient ice, attached to chains, also carved from ancient ice, formed the cogs and gears which pulled at the wooden doors.

Steel and other useful materials were hard come by in Glacia. And, cut off from most of the world, with no immediate trade partners, they were forced to make good of the land they lived on. North of Glacia, where the Sapphire Stream was at its narrowest, was a mass of ice that marks the end of it; strong as diamond. It was said that the ice came from the white dragon himself, from the age of the great feud. It was also said that it would remain in its crystallised state until the end of days, no matter how much the land heats, and only the flame of the red dragon was capable of melting it. It was at this narrowing, that the heat of the Sapphire Stream ended. The ice blocked the way to Athia. So, both Glacia and Athia remained separated by the extremes of the Sapphire Stream and an almost impenetrable block of ice. And, both Glacia and Athia remained unknown to the rest of the world, due to a large mountainous climb that encapsulates the whole of both lands, too high for any mortal to climb.

The Glacianne tribe made use of the ice by carving chunks of it away; the first of the tribe used the scattered sharpened pieces to extract it, as only the ice itself, can cut through it.

Freya and the younglings made a break for the gate as soon as it begun to open, as out in the open they were exposed. The watchtowers may have watched over the powdered snow plains surrounding the village, but they could not see what hid amongst the trees. Lying in wait, were usually hungry beasts looking to pounce on those unlucky enough to fall behind, or trip on their way back. It was usually a mad dash through the gate; however, guards were on standby awaiting the arrival of the younglings, and they were safely ushered back through.

***

Argon no longer had to carry Aylen, as her companion was already strong enough to be ridden. It had carried her from the cave, right down the perilous climb and back to the village.

Argon was behind the group of younglings and had ushered the rest down at a steady pace. They still looked as though they hadn't broken a sweat, possibly due to the fact that no Athianne ever did, as the heat would have evaporated any escaping perspiration immediately.

Athianne folk did not smell the greatest either; the extreme heat meant that water was seldom come by on the plains of Athia. However, they used special casks forged from the molten rock found all over their home. This rock seemed to have properties, that protected it from the steam that rose from the Sapphire Stream. They used these casks to extract steam from the stream and awaited its return back to water. This was mainly used for drinking and cooking, so they only washed when it was absolutely necessary. The smell of the villagers alone would have been an equally impressive deterrent to outsiders as the fort of the Glacianne tribe. However, on that day, the smell that was expelled from the village was unusually sweet. Everyone had washed and wore their best garments, ready for the festivities to begin.

The chief and the rest of the parents were awaiting their childs' safe return. The entrance to the village was wide open. Nothing but a few wildflowers, plants, and trees (no taller than the average adult Athianne), stood between the younglings and their families. The tallest structures around were the Athianne homes; large complex tent shaped structures forged from the molten rock and stone. Some of the tent structures, that were built centuries before, still stood in all their glory; more decorative than the Athianne homes, as they were used primarily for ceremonies and theatrical performances. It was the largest of these, that everyone had congregated in wait.

'Where is she?' the chief shouted with a deafening tone.

He moved his bear paw hands through the crowd of children and their companions before, surprisingly, he found his daughter to the back. 'There you are daughter.' He lowered his tone.

'Let me look at you. You already look like a leader little one. I am so proud of you. Now, let me see it. Which one of these fine creatures belongs to you?' he swayed his great head from side to side. His braided hair was woven into many a plait like thick silken ropes; it whipped the air with a swish when he moved. Everyone moved away. Leaving just Soria, still silent, stood in front of him. 'Well, daughter, where is it?' he looked less happy. 'Where is your companion?' he raised his tone, and blocked out the sun when he stood over her with the enormity of his shadow.

She huffed like a spoilt child and stepped to one side. Stood behind her, was the strange furry creature which came out of the cave.

He pointed his thick sausage finger at the creature. 'What is this?'

She replied softly, almost like a whisper. 'It's my companion.'

'Come again.' He scratched his bare chest. 'This is your companion? The companion of the future leader of the Athianne tribe. Ha ha!' he laughed eccentrically. 'Good one. Whose companion is this, Aylen's? Good joke daughter. I didn't know you had a humorous bone in your body.' The chief turned towards Aylen. 'So, you must be Soria companion?' he said and placed his hand out to pet the large wolf, which carried Aylen on its back.

The wolf's fur began to glow and it snarled angrily at him. Then, as he got closer, it bit the air in warning and growled louder.

He turned to Soria. 'Ha ha! It's got your attitude, that's for sure. It will have met its match with you, but I'm sure you will be up to the task of training it.'

'But, Father?' Soria begged her father to stop talking. She wasn't sure who would be embarrassed most, her father, or her. 'Please, listen to me!'

He continued to talk to himself, unaware of his daughters pleads. 'How kind it was of you to let it carry one of the lesser younglings on its back. That's what a true leader would do. We shall get ready for the great celebration. The ritual is fulfilled and our children have returned with their companions from the great guardian himself.' His voice rose even louder. 'And, my daughter has the most impressive companion of any future leader. Look at the size of that thing. Why, he's even bigger than Orange here.' He tapped his own companion on the shoulder, that stood at a third of his height. The large ape-like creature was not unlike that of an ordinary orangutan. But that was not the reasoning behind her name. When she wasn't walking around the village by the side of her keeper, the chief, she was sat around eating oranges in their dozens. The crowd had begun to cheer while the chief boomed his speech.

Soria let out a dreadful shriek and stomped her feet as she did so. This stopped everyone from cheering and her father looked at her. 'Do you wish to add something daughter?' he asked.

'Do you ever listen to a word I say?' she snapped. 'Will you shut your mouth so I can speak.'

Her father looked at her crossly, but, he was not permitted to speak until she had finished her outburst. 'This stupid thing is my companion. The guardian gave it to me. The wolf is not mine.'

He gave a strong look of concern. 'What?' he stepped closer to the creature beside her, and it jumped behind her leg.

'That thing is yours? Really? Tell to me the truth daughter, tell to me that you have received a strong companion, a chief's companion, and this is just a little joke?'

She looked down at her feet. Knowing she had already spoken out of turn to her father, she did not wish to push his patience. 'I am telling the truth.' She had begun to sob.

He stayed quiet for a minute, tilted his head from side to side and assessed the little furry thing. *What is it?* He thought, realising that he had not paid it much attention at all. He looked back at his daughter, who still had tears trickling from her eyes and was facing the floor.

The chief loved his daughter, more so than anyone or anything that had ever existed. He may have been a stern strong, leader, but his daughter upset was something he could not tolerate.

'Soria.' He said in a low affectionate tone. 'Soria, I am sorry.' He placed his forefinger under her chin and raised her head. 'It is okay. Maybe this creature is more impressive than can clearly be seen by the eye. It is in its infancy is it not? Maybe it will grow to be more than it now appears.' *Maybe, hopefully,* he thought.

She raised a slight smile. She believed her father's words like any daughter would. It was twice that this had been said to her that day, by two of the wisest of the Athianne, so she was beginning to believe it herself. It also reassured Argon, who too gave a sigh of relief.

She picked up the creature for the first time since she had laid eyes on it, and placed it carefully on her shoulder. It smiled at her a wide toothless grin, and she raised a half smirk back at it. 'Maybe you are right father. Maybe I have the strongest companion yet.'

'Why, of course I'm right!' he boomed. 'I am the chief; I am always right! Ha ha!'

He turned to the rest of the crowd who awaited permission to smile. He laughed aloud hysterically again and all began to cheer loudly. 'Let us make our way to the ceremonial tent. We shall begin this year's festivities right away!' he lifted his daughter on to his boulders for shoulders and everyone followed them into the tent.

***

'There you are my child,' said the chieftainess, mother of Ohmiya, 'I am so glad you made it back safely.'

Praise given to the guardian, thought Freya reminiscing on their journey upward. The return journey for the group, although just as perilous as the way there, was less so due to Ohmiya being preoccupied with Snowflake. His company seemed to keep her calm and she never strayed off path.

'She was no trouble whatsoever.' Freya spoke directly to the chieftainess, then louder at the crowd of parents. 'They were all mightily impressive, completed the ritual, and all received companions from our beloved guardian.'

The younglings were all embraced lovingly by their parents and showed off the mixture of creatures that they had returned with.

The chieftainess looked expectantly at her daughter, with eyes wide and hopeful. 'So where is it? Where is my daughter's companion?'

Freya tried to interject, 'If I might just say Nyssa…' But the chieftainess held up her hand for her to cease speaking.

'No you may not just yet Freya, I am trying to speak with my daughter. With respect to you, I appreciate what you have done, and you have done a mighty fine job bringing all our younglings home safe. But this is a moment I have been waiting for for a very long time.' She lowered her hand and turned back to Ohmiya.

'So, Ohmiya, daughter, show to me what the guardian saw fit to bestow upon our future leader.' She placed her hands together and wiggled her fingers like a child awaiting a treat.

'What do you mean mother? He's right here.' She gestured to her left and said, 'Meet Snowflake.'

The creature's fur was as white as snow and glistened the same way as the ground it stood upon. Difficult to see, as it looked camouflaged against the ground, it jumped into the arms of Nyssa. Her reflexes forced her to open her arms and catch him, but she looked stunned at the fuzzy ball with feet in her arms and dropped him to the floor. With his head planted in the deep snow, all you could see of the creature was his wiggling feet, and it flailing around for freedom.

'What did you do mother?' Ohmiya grabbed Snowflake and turned him upright.

'What is that thing?' Nyssa cried.

'I told you, he's Snowflake. The guardian gave him to me. Isn't he cute?'

Nyssa composed herself quickly in front of her tribe. She brushed herself down unnecessarily, cleared her throat and ran her hands down her hair. Her hair, like the rest of the tribe, was glitter white and coarse like straw; as she pushed down on it, it sprang back to its original shape. Unlike the wavy silken black hair of the Athianne tribe, Glacianne hair maintained its shape. It could not be styled, or altered, as it would spring back if it was moved. Some might say it looked like they wore icicles upon their heads.

'He's what now?' she was lost for a more astute answer.

Freya stepped in to offer her thoughts. 'I tried to explain Nyssa. The guardian seems to have offered Ohmiya, your daughter, a new kind of companion, a unique companion. Snowflake - *it pained her to say its name* – may not be entirely what he seems.' She thought long and hard about her next words, as she did not want to lie, but she wished not for the maddening of her leader. So, she embellished the truth a little to appease Nyssa. Although the arctic weather of Glacia was impossibly cold, she sensed the intense heat of the chieftainess' anger. 'Something magical happened when Ohmiya stepped up to the cave entrance, something extraordinary…'

'It did?' asked Ohmiya innocently.

'It did…' Freya responded sharply at her to stop her talking.

'Go on.' Said Nyssa.

Freya continued. 'The entrance seemed to gleam more impressively than I have ever seen it. It seemed to expel an energy that I have never felt before. It encompassed Ohmiya, it embraced her. Ohmiya seemed to be glowing in the same way that the cavern entrance did. As though she was one with the power of our guardian, as though the guardian had accepted her as something special.'

'It did?' asked Nyssa, eyes widened and pleased with the story so far, as that is what it was, a story.

'It did?' interjected Ohmiya.

'Yes, it did.' Freya said sternly through gritted teeth. 'Am I permitted to continue?' she asked Ohmiya rhetorically.

'Please go on.' Ordered Nyssa politely.

'There is not much more to it Nyssa. The light began to recede, and what was left was Ohmiya and Snowflake. Both of them glowing incandescently in the sunlight. It was truly wondrous to see, and it can be said with no degree of uncertainty, that something unprecedented happened at this year's ritual.'

Nyssa folded her arms and crinkled the skin between her eyebrows. She looked at Snowflake curiously and bent low to look at him. He smiled a toothless grin and moved closer to her. She was unsure if she saw him sparkle brighter than before; was it the story that made him seem more magical than before, or was it that she just willed it so for the sake of her daughter and the future of her tribe? Either way, Snowflake became less of a disappointment, and was now revered as a creature of mystery and intrigue.

Freya, defying the cold, began to sweat. Beads came from her forehead and froze instantly, which give her a lovely glow in the low sun.

'I always knew you were something special.' Said Nyssa, whilst admiring her daughter. 'And, now it has been proven, as our guardian also believes you are someone who deserves such a magical companion.'

Freya, a little shaken, which was rare for such an unwavering character, began to feel less worried. She said to herself that day, that what she had said was the truth. If she could convince herself that this was what happened, it would make it easier to continue the façade.

'This year's festivities are now particularly special. Not only has my own child, the future leader of the tribe, returned from the guardian's ritual unharmed. But the white dragon saw fit to bestow upon my daughter, a companion so unique, so incredible, that we do not even know what they will be capable of achieving together. On with the festivities, tonight we celebrate with conviction.'

Chapter Five

I t had been seven years since the festivities had occurred on that fateful day in both Glacia and Athia. All the younglings were reaching adulthood rapidly. Although it would be another five years before Ohmiya and Soria would assume their role as leader of their respective tribes, adulthood was considered to be thirteen.

The young adults of both sides of the Sapphire Stream were, as all young adults did until they reached thirteen, preparing for their lifelong professions amongst the rest of their people. The easiest, yet also most difficult of tasks, was to choose which path they would take. Aside from Ohmiya and Soria, whose paths were chosen for them through birth right, the others had but two choices: hunter/gatherer or watcher.

There was no need for healers, as all the tribes folk on either side generally lived ailment free. There was no need for engineers, as all that was already built, was all that they should have needed.

The Glacianne were able to fashion their own weapons if they so needed. The impressive architecture they resided behind was still standing from centuries before, with no need for repair or maintenance. The only need was a consistent collection of food and the watching of the wall that surrounded the tribe.

Likewise, the only necessary skillset required of the Athianne, was the ability to gather food. Different to that of the Glacianne, was that they gathered only plants and roots for food. Animals were deemed sacred and left to roam free; in return the animals left the Athianne alone, and even helped deter unwary young gatherers from the poisonous plant life.

The role of watcher was more a title than an actual role in Athia, with no known predators to cause concern, it simply allowed for those who had previously been gathering to rest and recuperate. They may not have needed to hunt down large creatures for food, like that of the Glacianne, but the Athianne needed to travel great distances across their land to retrieve enough food for the tribe. Glacianne need not venture far to track down an unsuspecting mammoth. They wandered dim-wittedly in vast numbers, and, were one to disappear from their numbers, the rest of the heard would not have known and continued on their march regardless.

Athia had not always been such a pleasant landscape. In the time shortly after the great battle of the dragons, the land was filled with vicious creatures with unholy features. Images of which are still carved into rock faces that are scattered around the land.

Sometimes teenage Athianne would use the images etched into the rocks as a means of telling tall tales. They would try to frighten the younglings with false fables; only for a spot of fun, as the older ones had done to them in their youth. But they would always explain that they were joking afterwards.

However, it was hard to frighten Soria with these tales when she was younger. As she relished the idea of such hideously aggressive creatures existing. She was particularly fond of a tale about the lycunflame; an ancient race of wolves with fangs that burnt as bright and hot as the sun itself. She liked to hear all the gory details of what they use to do to her ancestors, until a famous tribe leader named Validan made his name in history. He and his tribe were supposed to have forced such an evil creature to the very tops of the three mountains. They supposedly still lived there, and dared not venture back down for fear of his might.

But the story goes that, they, as well as all the other ancient predators of the land, feast on unsuspecting victims who dare venture up the mountains. Of course, that was just another story, and no one had ever known how much truth was in the tale. No Athianne had ever ventured farther than the entrance of the first mountain peak to collect their companion during the ritual. And, had the tribes folk believed such stories, they would not have let their young scale any of the peaks.

However, what drew Soria to this story when she was younger, is that Validan is supposedly a distant ancestor in her blood line. This again, was no more than hearsay, as they had no means of recording such details. Relatives were all but forgotten in her tribe as grandparents did not talk about their grandparents. No knowledge was needed to be passed on, as all they needed they had, and if they did not have it, they did not need it.

Soria was older now, though, and she too told tales to the younglings of Athia. However, she did so with vigour and held back no punches. Exactly seven years on from the day that she remembered all too well, the day that she was about to scale the mountain scape to receive her companion, she was telling a story of her own invention to the newly turned five-year olds of Athia.

The younglings held onto her every word, as she told them of the beasts in the mountains, how her distant relative, Validan, had turned them away from the land and slayed those who dared stay.

Obviously, Soria being Soria, she embellished massively and included details which would have suited a much older audience. She was on the verge of describing how he had the most fearsome of companions that battled by his side, and how the rest of their family had had the most fearsome of companions that Athia had ever witnessed, when a child spoke up.

'So, if your family has the most fearsome of companions, why did the guardian give you that?' she asked sheepishly.

'Hmm, ermm…' She was lost for words, which was unusual for Soria, as she usually had an answer for everything. 'Why do you believe him not to be as fearsome as any other of the companions bestowed upon my family?' her forehead crinkled angrily.

The young girl was unable to speak in fear of what Soria might do. Although she had mellowed marginally over time, she was still as intimidating as ever.

A boy, who seemed less concerned, spoke up. 'He's just so cute and fuzzy. He doesn't look like he could hurt anything.' Then he stroked his fur. Soria's companion began to tap its foot like a happy bunny and smiled a wide toothless smile. 'He doesn't even have any teeth.' The boy continued.

Soria, whose legs were crossed on the floor, stood with conviction and then leaned over the boy. 'Ah, that's just what he wants you to believe; that he is unable to do any harm, that he is just a cute fuzzball. But, when you least expect it, and when he sees you all alone…' She bent low and stared the boy dead in the eyes, so that he dare not blink. 'Then… He attacks!'

All the kids screamed hysterically and ran off to the ceremonial tent. She laughed so hard, that she never noticed Solis stood behind her. She was walking toward the tent, as she had done seven years before, when Soria was awaiting the yearly ritual to begin.

'You know, at this time of year, it is, I, that is supposed to be telling the younglings a story.'

Soria jumped up as though the ground was electrically charged and glared at Solis. 'You frightened me.'

'Ha, frightened you. I did not think that to be possible. Besides, it serves you right for frightening the little ones. At this time of year, that pleasure should be mine alone.'

'I just warmed them up for you.' Said Soria with a smirk.

Solis raised an eyebrow at her and spoke to her in a grandmotherly way. 'You should spend less time scaring the little ones with tall tales, and spend more time with your companion. You should be preparing for your role, for when you assume your place as, Chieftainess of the Athianne tribe. And, if that is something that sounds too taxing, you could at least name him. The poor creature goes by many names around these parts: *Useless Ball of Fluff, Fluffball, Scraggy Puff, and Mr. Fuzzy.*'

Soria interrupted her. 'That's it.'

Solis scratched her head. 'What's it?' she asked.

'That's it.' She replied. 'That's his name, the one you just said.
Mr. Fuzzy.'

'Mr. Fuzzy?' Solis thought she was joking, until she repeated it.

'Mr. Fuzzy is perfect, I don't know why, but it just works.' She
said in a sarcastic tone.

'But, it's not a warrior's name, nor the name of a warrior's
companion. It will not strike fear into those who wish to attack us.'

'And Orange does? Look around you, Solis.' Soria said as she
waved her arms around eccentrically. 'Who does it need to strike
fear into. The sunflowers. Or, perhaps the daffodils. It is no wonder
the guardian offered me such a pathetic companion to lead our tribe
with. Our purpose in this world is meaningless. We do not need to
protect our people from anything and we do not need worry about
anything ever. We live, we get a magical pet; although, why we need
to scale the mountain for one when there are numerous creatures
around us that would serve us just fine, is something that eludes me.
We gather food, we eat, and finally we grow old and die. Except for
you maybe. Just how old are you anyway?'

The usually composed Solis was feeling less generous with her
good nature and raised a hand to Soria. 'How dare you? I am a
tolerant woman, I truly am. But you push me too far sometimes
child.'

Soria looked shocked at her outburst. A threat, no matter how
benign against a member of the chief's family, would have certainly

meant death. But, Solis was the exception to the rule. Should she have had to raise her hand to anyone, the chief might take action on that person instead, as Solis was revered amongst the tribe. Soria did not know the reason, and maybe she did not need to know the reason right there and then. She just knew that she had overstepped her place, and apologised repeatedly.

'I am sorry Solis, truly I am, it was not my place to speak to you this way.'

'You're damn right it wasn't your place.'

Soria stared at her feet, which Solis had only seen her do a handful of times in the past. 'Listen child. You are still a child, regardless of what our laws state, and you will be learning for many years to come. Even when you are grown, you will be continually learning. But, at some point, in the not so distant future, you will understand your place in this world, as I have come to learn mine. But, with all my years of wisdom, I still do not know everything, and I will eventually pass on to the next life, not knowing a great many things. Such is life.'

Soria looked up and smiled. A humble look was seldom seen on Soria's face. But, Solis new exactly what to say to bring out the best in her.

'Now, you and Mr. Fuzzy move out of my way.' She rolled up her sleeves and winked at Soria. 'I have some whipper snappers to scare. If you haven't knocked all the scare out of them.'

Soria moved out of the way for her and her ridiculously large garments that she wore every single year. 'Mind the trailing dress.' Said Solis.

'Why can't you just wear a smaller dress?' whispered Soria.

'I heard that.' Shouted Solis from inside the ceremonial tent.

Soria took a deep look into Mr. Fuzzy's eyes. 'So, after seven years you have embarrassed me irrevocably in front of the rest of the tribe, shown off no useful or interesting skills, yet I am stuck with you. So, let us find out what you can do.'

For some reason, giving her companion a name, no matter how ridiculous, allowed Soria to finally feel some kind of connection to him. She looked at him, not quite lovingly, but differently to how she had done before. Less like an unwanted gift, and more like something that was alive, with feelings. It smiled at her a large toothless grin and stroked up against her leg.

'Let's not get ahead of ourselves.' She said to him. 'I'm still not in that place yet. But I will entertain talking to you, and possibly letting you be within a metre of me.'

Soria had not yet fully accepted that Mr. Fuzzy was useless, as she still wished that he would be capable of something extraordinary. She had not yet completely accepted him as her companion, but had not yet given up hope, that he was not all that he could be.

The other younglings who scaled the mountain with her, had companions that had grown somewhat over the years. Some were even developing remarkable abilities. Aylen's wolf, Torch, could burn like a flame and was hot to touch, even to the Athianne. However, his flame could not burn Aylen. She could ride upon him as though charging through the village on a ball of fire, but his flame was harmless to her. Training of a companion was uniquely delivered by each keeper and irreplicable. One might say that it wasn't always the keeper that was doing the training. Torch seemed to have unearthed a quality in Aylen; a hidden strength that may have forever laid dormant had it not been for their pairing. Soria often thought about having a companion with such an ability, especially when she was looking at Mr. Fuzzy. But, after speaking to Solis, if only for a brief moment, she finally bonded with her own companion.

***

Freya had just arrived back from an all-day hunting trip, smelling of death. The fur coat she wore was stained with the blood of a large deer. It hung lifeless over the back of her companion, who was panting rigorously. 'Come here boy, drop it there.' Freya pointed to the ground in front of her, and two watchers came over and carried away the carcass.

Ohmiya ran over and wrapped her arms around her. She had grown up a lot over the last seven years, but Freya still towered over her. 'Little Ohmiya, look at you! You are getting big. Step back, let me have a look at you.'

'I'm the same size I was when you saw me last. We don't live that far apart and you see me every fourth sunrise.' Said Ohmiya.

Freya gestured for Ohmiya to walk with her and they strolled slowly back toward the town. The town within Glacia was not as humble as the open village and scattered tents of Athia. It was a thriving city, that had been crafted within the shed scales of the guardian dragon. It was a large ominous entrance into the Glacianne tribes civilisation. Within the wooden pikes, which form the towns outer walls, was an impossibly large dragon skin. It was completely hollow, from where the dragon had slid out of it and emerged in its new skin. The structure was hard as diamond, and kept out the cold and all other weathers that attempted to breach it; all but the light of the sun, which shone magnificently through the scales, so it was as bright inside as it was out. This also gave it a warm cosy feel.

Freya and Ohmiya walked through the gaping mouth which formed the entrance and into the belly of the beast. Inside, it was unrecognisable as the interior of a dragon. Structures had been erected within it from fallen timber. There were homes, food halls and armouries. The Glacianne did not have currency, so shops were not necessary. Anything found was kept by its finder and people hardly ever traded. So there were no shops, or stalls to purchase goods of any kind. Everything that was needed was shared and anything else was unnesseccary. They did have structures that were used for theatre productions and plays, as the Glacianne liked to entertain. Plays would often be performed, with no invite, or ticket necessary.

The stories that were performed, were less tall tales like those told in Athia, and more tales of great warriors that existed since before the time of their existence. As, unlike the Athianne, the Glacianne liked to record the past.

Carvings were etched into great slabs of ice that stood in the centre of the village. Some told stories of times gone by, and others were used as a way to remember those who were no longer with them. The Glacianne people liked to believe, that everyone was born equal, and left this world equal to those who had left before them. So instead of an individual grave marker, they used the same one. Obviously not everyone's name can fit on just one. So, there were five that existed at that time. Each of those great ice slabs hosted thousands of names. When loved one's paid tribute to those they had lost, they were also paying tribute to others within the tribe. This tradition was important to the Glacianne tribe, as it allowed those who no longer had any offspring to be forever remembered. The Glacianne way of life was dependant on the sacrifices, and the work that their ancestors put into the construction of their civilisation. So, to not remember those who had passed away many lives before their own began, in the same way as those who had been lost recently, would have been an intolerable notion.

'Where is Snowflake? Freya said to Ohmiya, as they stood by the memorial ice slabs. I thought that he followed you everywhere?' Freya placed her head against the largest one and whispered something silently. Her companion also leaned in and placed its head against the ice. It was like they were in sync with one another. She rarely spoke to the wolf, that was unnamed and always with her, unless she was in company, yet it always seemed to know exactly what she wanted it to do.

Ohmiya looked up at Freya 'He's with my father. He thinks that he can unleash his inner potential. I keep telling him that I like him just the way he is. My mother does not seem bothered by it, but I can tell my father is worried. As chieftainess, I will no doubt live the rest of my days behind these walls anyway. So, why I need a stronger companion I don't know. He's perfect as he is.'

Freya turned to Ohmiya concernedly and let out a sigh. 'Your father is right to worry for you. If not for your age, you may feel differently too. The outside world is less predictable than within the safety of our walls. It can change rapidly. Our enemies may not always be the carnivorous animals that skulk around just a few hundred feet away.'

Ohmiya, half listened to what Freya was saying, and too placed her head against the ice-cold slabs and pretended to whisper something. Freya smiled at her, knowing that she was whispering gibberish, though she appreciated her attempt at respecting those in the afterlife. Freya started whispering gibberish too, jokingly.

Ohmiya laughed. 'I was just paying my respects.' She said.

Freya laughed also. 'And I'm sure the spirits appreciate your waffling.'

'What are you saying to them, to those you have lost?' Ohmiya looked genuinely interested. 'My parents won't tell me what I am supposed to say. I see people whispering things for most of the day, but I do not know what they say.'

Freya placed her hand on Ohmiya's shoulder and lent down next to her, to meet her eye level. She spoke in a low affectionate tone. 'The reason they do not tell you what to say, is because it is something you must discover alone. Only you can know what to say to those you have lost. And, the reason you do not know what to say yet, is because you have not lost anyone important to you yet. They don't tell you, to try shield you from that pain that you will inevitably have to embrace. It is not something a child needs to know. You may be soon considered an adult, yet you are not quite ready to be burdened with the weight of that which comes with age. When you are older, you will know what to say. And, when you speak words of comfort to a dear one you have lost, you can aim that to others that have also passed on, so they too are comforted by your words.'

'Oh, I see.' Ohmiya nodded with agreement, but she was not entirely sure what Freya meant.

They had begun to walk towards Ohmiya's home, and they did so in relative silence. Just the squelching of their shoes was all that could be heard. All the Glacianne wore the same boots, which they learnt to make for themselves from as young as four; just as they did all their other clothes, which they learnt from a young age to make for themselves. Mammoth, although used for food, were also used as a resource for other Glacianne products. Their skin was tough and thick; so thick it could repel cold like a magnet. So, shoes, coats and other garments were crafted from it.

The mammoth skin shoes made a very distinct squelching noise. It was loud and sounded like those who wore them were walking through a muddy bog.

Ohmiya spoke abruptly to break the silence. 'Why should I worry about our enemies changing? No one can breach the Sapphire Stream and no one has ever been able to get over the high stone wall that goes around us. So, all we have to worry about are the creatures, don't we?'

Freya sighed. 'This is a story that is not mine to tell.' She pointed at Ohmiya's door. It may have been home to the little, future Chieftainess, but it was humble, and no more extravagant than any other home. It was just positioned further back from the entrance to the city. Should anything have breached the walls, their home would be last to fall. 'You're home, you should go inside. You should not spend too much time away from Snowflake, especially not at this stage.'

'He's fine.' Ohmiya smiled. 'My father is bonding with him, too.'

Freya sniffed in discontent. 'Remember this, if you remember anything I tell you. It is not anyone else, but you alone who can bring out Snowflake's true potential.'

Freya left her at the door and walked away without saying goodbye. Ohmiya shrugged her shoulders and bounced through the door. 'I'm back.' She shouted.

Ohmiya's father was stood in the centre of the room waving his hands in front of Snowflake. He was an impossibly large man, who had to remain bent over in his own home in fear of scraping his head on the ceiling. This meant that he walked with a permanent slump, but he still towered over almost all others. His voice shook the walls and echoed throughout the city.

'I'm going to attack you.' He said to Snowflake. 'You need to defend yourself by any means necessary.' He paused, then shouted, and charged. 'Ah! I've got you now.'

He ran at him and stooped down to grab him. Snowflake launched himself into the air, quite energetically for a creature with no visible legs, and landed on his shoulder. Then, opened his mouth as wide as he could, a large tongue came out and licked the cheek of the chief.

The chief let out an almighty laugh and collapsed to the floor, which rumbled, lifting Ohmiya from her feet for a brief moment. Snowflake continued to tickle the chief with his tongue until he called out in submission.

Ohmiya laughed aloud. 'Great work father. It seems you have turned him into a voracious killing machine.'

Snowflake hopped off of the chief and ran over to Ohmiya like a puppy. It rubbed its bristly fur against her leg affectionately and purred like a cat.

'It seems, daughter, that I have been unsuccessful today. Maybe we shall try again another day. I am sure he can do something, other than smile.'

Snowflake smiled at Ohmiya, she picked him up from the ground rubbed her forehead against his. 'But, that is your superpower isn't it Snowflake.'

Her father moved through the house like a bewildered beast and scratched his head. 'It will not be enough, if he is to protect you against threats from the outside.'

'What threats? I have been outside the walls before and I have been fine. I will do it again, and I will be fine again. Plus, nothing can breach these walls, as we cannot even knock them down ourselves. Nothing will happen to us, so long as the guardian watches over us?'

Ohmiya's father sat in his chair on the far side of the room. As he fell harshly onto the seat, the house shook. 'Sit little one.' He said.

Ohmiya sat on the floor in front of him and crossed her legs in anticipation. Her eyes locked on her father in admiration. He took in a deep breath, flared his nostrils and let out a sigh. 'Life is not everlasting my child.'

'I know that father.' She interjected. He held his hands up for her to keep silent while he finished.

'Life for everything, is not everlasting. The trees may seem like they could live forever, but they eventually die. As do the plants, the bugs, the creatures and people.' He stopped and looked up to the ceiling. Then, he continued. 'The guardian dragon has not been seen in my lifetime, nor has it been seen by anyone in generations. The only reason we know of its existence, is because of the city we live in that was formed from its scales, and the stories that we have passed down through the ages. But, one thing that is not spoken of, is the life of a dragon. That is because, no one has ever seen a dragon, so no one knows how long one might live. This home that our people created hundreds of years ago, relies solely on these walls remaining intact. But, if the stories are true, it will fall when the white dragon falls. If the story is true, and he still lives upon the topmost cave at the edge of Glacia, then his life may soon be up. It may well last for centuries more, but we cannot be certain. It is this burden that the chief of this tribe has to bear. If our city should fall, the people would look to us for guidance, wisdom and strength. If that time should arise while you lead this tribe, then it is you, with the help of your companion, that will lead the Glacianne tribe to safety, so they can once again prosper. If Snowflake can do little more than make others smile, he would not be fit for this role. And, the people may question; is its keeper fit for hers?'

Ohmiya still smiled with blissful ignorance. She had listened to her father's words, as though she would a bedtime story, and not words of warning.

'So, take Snowflake, train him with the others and their companions. Your leadership, and the future of this tribe may one day depend on it.'

Ohmiya stood up righteously and placed her hands on her hips. 'Right father, I will.' She said in a mocking tone. 'Come on Snowflake. Let us unleash your inner power.' She laughed jokingly, Snowflake hopped onto her shoulder and they exited the house with a burst of energy.

Her father placed his head in hands and sighed. He knew that his free-spirited child would most likely fail to see the warning in his tale. But, he had hoped she would seem less oblivious to the fact that his words were true.

All things live and all things die; such is life. But Ohmiya, at only twelve, failed to grasp the magnitude of this concept. Life is ever lasting to a child, and so why wouldn't a dragon, who was regarded as a deity, outlive her and her people.

Chapter Six

'I never thought I would say this Aylen,' Soria said
with her head stooped low, 'but Mr. Fuzzy and I
require your assistance with our training.'

It had been almost five years since Soria had made any effort at
bonding with her companion. She was rapidly approaching her time
to assume her role as Chieftainess of the Athianne people. The
Athianne, nor the Glacianne, chief waited for their time to end before
they appointed a successor. Should the Chief have a child, and should
that child reach the right age to assume the role, the mantel is passed
on. This gave the successor the chance to take advice from their

former leader and parent, especially during the early stages of their time as chief.

Soria was ready to ascend to the role, but Mr. Fuzzy was no more fit for the role as a chief's companion, than he was on the day he was gifted to her. She had made the effort to participate in play with the other younglings she had grown up around. But, she made as little contact as possible. Her activities with them were more a source of research. She spied on other companions abilities, to see if she too could awaken the same ones within Mr. Fuzzy. For she feared that his only ability was to be a doting smile of affection. Which, to Soria's discontent, she loved and hated in equal measure.

She stayed away from one child in particular as she grew into the young woman she was becoming. That person was Aylen. By far, Aylen had the most impressive companion. The wolf she received from the red dragon had grown to stand six feet on all fours. He was developing new and interesting abilities on a bi-yearly basis. Torch, without question, was the companion of a leader. And, Soria hated her for it. Although, *and she would never admit it,* she could not have given up Mr. Fuzzy, she still resented others who had companions that exceeded her own in power.

'You know that's the first time you have spoken to me since we were five.' Said Aylen, who had grown somewhat unexpectedly in the last two years. She had grown from a small sickly child, into a tall, rather striking featured, young woman. No longer passive, she said what she wished to say with conviction, unafraid of anyone. Torch, who stood under her arm and looked piercingly at Soria, gave her an unbound confidence.

The girls stood eye to eye with one another, as Soria was quite tall for age too. 'I know I haven't. I have been preoccupied trying to discover if Mr. Fuzzy here is capable of more than grinning intolerably.' Mr. Fuzzy then smiled at both Aylen and Torch, which forced a smile from them both.

'His smiles are infectious, though, I've got to admit.' Said Aylen.

Both girls broke into an awkward laughter and then stopped abruptly.

Aylen spoke freely. 'You have always thought yourself better than me, than any of us. Why should we help you?'

'I am your future leader; you should do as I ask unwaveringly. It is our way.' Soria ordered.

'You are no future leader of mine. I look out for my family and the good of the tribe. I do not need a, born entitled, telling me what to do.' Snapped Aylen.

Soria stepped forward angrily and raised her finger. She had begun to speak. 'How dare you talk to me in that way. I ....' She took one step too close to Torch, who ground his teeth, snarled, then snapped its jaws only an inch away from her pointing finger.

Aylen smiled smugly. 'You'll... what exactly? Anyone takes a stab at me, will feel the wrath of Torch. Not even your father has a companion that can match him in combat. I can do and say as I please and no one will ever poke fun of me, or threaten me ever again. Not least of all you. So, no, I will not help you. You and Mr. Fuzzy be on your way will you. You are ruining mine and Torch's morning run.'

Aylen hopped onto the huge wolf and told him to stay for a minute, as she stroked its royal red coat. 'You never know, they might appoint me chieftainess of the tribe in place of you. That way I will have helped you anyway. You will not have to bear the burden of the title, with such a worthless creature beside you.' She spat on the floor before her feet. 'You are not fit for ruling the Athianne. And, you never were.'

Aylen had gone from sight in a burst of light that came from Torch. His speed was unparalleled.

Soria was left looking to the floor. She had never been spoken to in such a way, and even though she knew she deserved some of what was said, she did not ever think any would dare speak the words aloud. She was broken. Her heart ripped from within her and trodden into the ground. She was so sure of herself, that she shunned all else around her. She was without friends and without a strong companion. Her entitlement to lead had overshadowed her ability to think of anything other than asserting her authority on others. She had not dreamt of anyone contesting her right to rule, and she assumed that friendships were her god given right. *Everyone would want to be around me, regardless of how she behaved,* she had often thought growing up. But, as it happened, she couldn't have been more wrong.

***

It had become unseasonably warm in Glacia, as all seasons in Glacia were usually indistinguishable from one another. The sun rose higher and hotter in summer, but the heat never reached the surface and the people never felt the warmth of its rays. It was no longer the squelching of the Glacianne footwear that could be heard as people pottered around, but splashing as they walked over a small layer of water that rested neatly upon the snowy surface.

This alone would not have been a concern, but only a week before, had the ground shook uncontrollably for several minutes. The unprecedented earthquake caused destruction across the whole of Glacia, which could be seen all the way up to the white dragons cave. Trees lay flat to the ground, like an evergreen pathway. Those that used the trees for shelter could be seen by the watchers, fighting over what little cover was left. The wolves that hid close by could no longer hide amongst the bushes. This was a welcomed treat for watcher and hunter alike. The watchers could see farther afield than before and the hunters did not need to hunt, as many an animal had fallen victim to the tremble. Deer lay flattened under fallen ferns and mammoth were trapped under the boulders.

The Glacianne hunters were not vicious killers, and felt a great deal of empathy to those that had fallen. They were, after all, people who lived peacefully alongside animals. There was far too much food for them alone, and so they carried the remaining dead to the opening in front of the Glacianne city. The offering of food was for the wolves that usually lurked on the outskirts. This seemed to deter them from going after the Glacianne hunters, which made for a relatively restful week. The wolves, after all, were simply trying to feed their own pack, so they were not regarded as evil, and were respected as well as feared.

The bizarre weather that followed, however, unnerved the tribe elders. Meetings were held frequently in secret. The young were pushed to play with one another in the larger structures, that were usually reserved for ceremonies and large productions.

Ohmiya, who was now only a week away from seventeen and the ceremony that would place her as leader of the Glacianne tribe, was being excluded from the secret meetings. She, and the rest of the young adults were only told what the elders thought was necessary for them to know, and never told more than they thought was needed. Ohmiya was still a little free spirited and less worried about things that would concern others, yet even she knew that something was amiss.

She was still scheduled to take on her role, as no plans had changed, but her mother and father had been less than honest with her up until that point.

Her father bulldozed through the door as he always did. For only the fifth time that year, it came off the hinges, hit the side wall and dropped to the floor. He stooped down low and picked it up, placed it back in its rightful place, then gave himself a nod for a job well done.

'What happens when mother wants to come in?' The chief jumped and bashed his head harshly on the ceiling, which very nearly took flight. 'Or, what if I wish to leave. That door won't work if you just stick it back it its place off its hinges. We would be better off making it an opening, or making a thick curtain from mammoth skin if you continue to burst through like a raging yack.'

The chief, still swatting invisible stars that floated around his head, scratched the newly forming bump on his head. 'I didn't see you there daughter, what are you doing sneaking up on an old man like that.' He said, slightly irritated.

'Maybe the reason you jumped so energetically, is because it is you that has been doing all the sneaking around lately father.' Ohmiya folded her arms accusingly and smiled a wide smile, then stamped her left foot impatiently. Snowflake was stood beside her, still the same size as he was when he was first gifted to me. He, too, stomped his foot and mimicked his keepers actions.

'I do not know what you are talking about. You are paranoid. I do not sneak.' He walked past her and tried going into the next room in the modest sized wooden hut.

Ohmiya stepped in his way, and continued to stamp her foot, this time a little harder, and crossed her arms a little tighter. 'Of course not, that would require stealth, but you are as stealth like as a baby mammoth, in the open snow, with a bell strapped around its neck as it walks.'

The chief moved his daughter firmly to one side, by lifting her at the shoulders and removing her from the ground, then placing her gently to one side. She could not have hoped to wriggle free from his bear grip. 'Have care how you speak to me, you are not chieftainess yet and you still live under my roof. When you take your place as leader of the tribe, and you have grown under the weight of the responsibility, you can advise me on what I should and should not be doing.' He grunted at her.

Ohmiya, at nearly seventeen, had grown rather tall. She still had the innocent face of a child, but she stood at least six feet tall. Her hair was glitter white, coarse like straw and grew thickly, down and outward. Her eyes were an ocean blue shade, like that of the rest of the Glacianne people. However, hers replicated the shimmer of the Sapphire Stream, and seemed to swirl constantly.

She raised her voice ever so slightly. 'That is my point father. If I am to take my place as the chieftainess of this tribe, I need to know exactly what is going on. And, there is definitely something going on. I cannot begin my time as leader, if I do not know all that is happening in the land we live in. You need to tell me why you are meeting with the other elders, and have done so for the last week.

He stopped in the entrance between the living area and the kitchen. He exhaled eccentrically, 'I suppose I can't keep this from you anymore. I am no good at keeping secrets at the best of times, but this is too large of a secret to keep from the future leader of our tribe.'

He turned and dropped heavily into his chair, and his daughter who was now too large to sit cross legged, sat on the chair on the opposite side of the room.

'What is it father?' She asked with concern in her voice.

'Do you remember what I said to you five years ago, about the white dragon?'

'Not really, you told me a lot of stories when I was a youngling. I do not recall all of the details of every story.' Ohmiya replied.

The chief looked unsurprised. 'I thought as much. Anyway, I was telling you about how life does not go on forever, and that everything has a beginning and an end.'

Ohmiya raised an eyebrow. 'Yes, what does that have to do with anything?'

The chief raised his tone. 'It has everything to do with anything! Things have been happening in Glacia recently, things that have not been seen before. Snow is melting, the Sapphire Stream is warming, and even the creatures that reside outside the walls of our city are behaving differently.'

'What are you saying father?' She asked with concern.

'I am saying, that the only explanation is that something has happened to the white dragon. The elders disagree because our city's walls still stand, but I fear it is only a matter of time before they begin to fall.'

Ohmiya gasped in horror, and stood like a scornful teenager who had just been told something she did not wish to hear. 'That cannot be it, not ever, especially not now. What are we to do? What are the people to do? Oh no, this cannot be happening, they are going to look to me for wisdom. I am not even chieftainess yet, and I am certainly not gifted with the wisdom that is required to lead us out of such a calamity. What am I to do father? What am I to do?'

Ohmiya was in her father's personal space, gasping and panting, struggling for every breath. He placed his mighty hands in hers, and spoke with a deep soothing tone. 'That, my child, is what we have been trying to figure out. Do not worry, though, as this is why you rule with me and your mother by your side, until you are old enough to make decisions for yourself. This is why it is not in the event of my demise, that a chief's child becomes coronated. When you are older, wiser, and you have a partner to stand by your side, like I have your mother, you can lead our tribe unaided. Until then, I will be with you every step of the way. We can get through this so long as we have each other; and your mother of course, as alas, I do not make any decisions without consulting her first. In fact, half the decisions I make are based on her ideas. But that, my daughter, is one secret I would like us to keep.'

The chief winked at his daughter. He could feel her tiny hands in his, go from a tremor, to a steady shake, and then still. He had comforted her, as a he always had as a child. Ohmiya looked up to her father with the same regard she did the white dragon.

'Thanks father, I do not know what I would do without you.' Ohmiya gave her father a huge hug.

He embraced her lovingly and smiled. 'Well, let us hope that I am around for a great many years. You still have a lot of growing up to do and I still have a whole lot of parenting to do.'

'So what is the plan, if the walls fall?' Ohmiya persisted for an answer to the pending problem.

'Well, in the event that our walls begin to crumble, it is my duty as chief of this tribe to find out what is causing the problem. So, I will scale the mountain with my companion while our people are still safe behind these walls. I will go up to the cave where the white dragon lays slumber and I will find out what to do from there.'

The chief's companion was a white bear with barbs for fur. It was as large as he was, so it stayed outside for the most part. It could not be in the house at the same time as he, as the house would have no longer stood. And no one else would have been able to enter, as there would not be enough room to move around. It truly was a companion for a chief, and their presence was known when they walked around the city. Every step they took made a mini quake. They were not feared, though, as his companion was more a giant teddy bear than a vicious animal. It would protect the chief with its life, but it would much rather play with the younglings than fight given a choice.

'But what if it occurs when I become leader? Will that task not then fall into my hands?' Ohmiya looked scared.

'Well in that eventuality, it will be my duty as a father as well as former chief, to scale the mountain and find out what is going on. Either way, it will not be something that you should concern yourself with.'

Ohmiya gave her father another loving squeeze and then let him go. 'You should go then father. You should plan with the rest of the elders. I will not bother you with my questions. I will simply follow your guidance. I am sure that everything will be fine.'

'Indeed it will daughter. But for now, let us eat. All this plotting and planning has made me hungry as an ox.'

'You are hungry six times a day father.' Ohmiya laughed, and so too did her father. He wrapped his arm around her shoulder and they made their way into the kitchen.

***

It was less than a week before Soria was to assume her role as the Chieftainess of the Athianne tribe. The once ready and raring to lead Soria, was all but lost. Training of a companion was something that was supposed to come naturally to the people. There were no set guidelines, no classroom teachings and no one to turn to aside from parents. Because each companion was completely unique to its keeper, there was no way of documenting what to do and when.

The Glacianne, too, *usually* led the way with this approach, and although they like to mark down their past and those that had passed away before them, they made no attempt to teach their younglings how to raise their companions.

Raising your companion was, in itself, a rite of passage. If you could not train your own companion, then no one would have done it for you.

Soria was inconsolable, sat by herself on the outskirts of the village. Solis, as she often turned up unexpectedly, walked by. She watched as Soria sobbed; droplets fell from her eyes and evaporated as soon as they hit the ground. She was hunched over and did not see Solis arrive, until she placed her hand gently upon her back.

'Well, I never thought I would see the day.' Solis spoke softly and sympathetically. 'Although there is no doubt in my mind, that what has caused you to feel like this is incontestably of your own doing.'

Soria looked up and scowled at Solis. ' Watch the tone of your face with me young one.' Solis said to her.

Soria placed her head back into her crossed arms and continued to sob a little harder than before. Solis bent down and sat on the tree stump next to her. She began to rub her back gently to comfort her. 'Well, it must be bad. It is usually the others I am comforting after they have bumped into you. What could have possibly made you feel this way?'

'You wouldn't understand.' Soria replied sharply.

'Ah. I see. Well, in all my years of living, never have I heard such a thing leave a teenagers lips.' She said sarcastically. 'In all my years of existence, I must not have come across a problem as profound as that of a sixteen-year-old girl. Maybe I should retrieve one of the younglings for you to confide your problem too.' Solis said.

Soria stopped sobbing and stared deeply into Solis's eyes. They were kind, forgiving eyes. The longer she looked into them, the quicker she began to stop feeling sorry for herself and feel a little better. Without so much as a word shared between them, Soria had calmed herself.

'How do you do that?' Soria asked.

'Do what my child?' She replied with a grin, knowing what she was referring to, but wishing to hear the answer anyway.

Soria smiled back. 'You know what. It doesn't seem to matter how upset someone is, you seem to manage to set their mind at ease. It's like you have a superpower or something.'

Solis laughed at the notion of possessing powers of any sort, although she did not deny the possibility. 'I don't know, perhaps it is the face of an elderly woman that is hard to disappoint? The only thing disappointing to an elderly person like myself is seeing sadness in the young. So, what is it that has you so upset? And, let us see if we can resolve the matter.'

Soria looked reluctant to share, not least because she did not wish to show weakness, but mainly because she did not confide anything in anyone. Emotion was weakness in her eyes. But, it was hard to decline Solis. Her inviting voice compelled the listener to reveal their secrets willingly.

'I guess I always thought at this stage in my life, right before I was about to named chieftainess of the tribe, I would be in a more sturdy position. Everyone hates me, my companion is... Well look at him.' She gestured toward Mr. Fuzzy, who was perched next to her smiling gormlessly. She stroked his fuzzy fur and looked hopelessly at Solis for an answer to an unasked question, then continued. 'What do I do? Where do I go from here? I don't feel fit to lead. How can I accept the role as leader of this tribe, when some of the people are unwilling to follow me? How do I prove myself worthy?'

'Ah, now that is the right question.' Solis looked impressed. 'This is a different Soria, to the one that I have known all these years. Only someone who is ready to lead, would ask such a question.'

'What do you mean?' Soria questioned.

Solis whipped a forming tear from the corner of Soria's eye, and stroked back the strays of her silken black hair, which covered her face. 'Well, you asked; how do I prove myself worthy? One who believes it is the people who have to prove themselves worthy in the presence of their leader, is not fit to lead. But, one who believes it is their duty to prove themselves worthy of leading, is someone who is worth following.

'Just because a person is born into a position, does not mean they are deserving of it. So, it is the responsibility of that person to prove themselves worthy of that position in the eyes of the people. In some ways, it is harder for those born into power, than it is for those of a humble upbringing who gain it. Those who are born with it, have to constantly prove they are worthy of it. Whereas, those who gain it, never have to prove their worth again.'

Soria looked intrigued. 'So, how do I prove my worth to the people?'

Solis gave a slight chuckle and begun to shuffle forward from where she was sat. 'That my child, is a question only you can find the answer to, and something I cannot help you with.' She was struggling to stand as she spoke, so Soria offered her a hand. 'Besides which, I cannot stay out in this heat any longer. Either my age is becoming something of a nuisance to my daily routine, or the weather is changing, which would be even more worrying. We haven't had a shift in climate in my lifetime, and that my child, has been longer than I care to think about.'

'You are right; it is getting eerily hot around here, and we can usually endure the intense heat of Athia without a care. What do you think could be the cause?' Soria asked.

Solis looked at Soria and smiled. 'Maybe that is a task for our future leader to take on; a mystery to solve, perhaps? It could have something to do with what is happening on the other side of the Sapphire Stream. This world, the part of it we live in anyway, relies on a delicate balance between our side and theirs.' Said Solis.

'I haven't ever heard you talk about the other side of the Sapphire Stream before, not really anyway. Just that it exists, and the people, not too dissimilar to ourselves, look to the white dragon as their guardian, as their god.' Said Soria.

'That's right, yet there is far more to the tale than that. It has never been necessary to talk about until now, but I suppose I could give you a little more to go on, now you are coming of age.

'As it is our weather that gets hotter and not colder, one can only assume it is to do with their guardian. You see, as the red dragon sleeps atop the mountain scape, his every breath is almost as hot as the fire he breathes. That is why we made our home way down here, away from the mountain peaks. As you would no doubt have noticed, the heat rises the closer you get to the peaks. The lowest peak, the first peak, is as far as we have usually ventured, because our bodies are not designed to withstand such temperatures. The heat from his breath, heats the water of the Sapphire Stream, which is why it would scorch the skin of those who are stupid enough to touch it.

'On the other side of the Sapphire Stream resides a tribe, very different from our own, yet almost definitely the same. Their weather system is much, much colder than ours. This is only known, because on very, very clear days, the white tips of the cave from the story, where the white dragon is presumed to slumber, can be seen from Athia. It is said that his very breath would freeze the flesh on your bones. His breath flows through the forests on the other side of the Sapphire Stream, until it reaches the water itself. It would instantly freeze if not for the red dragon. Should anything happen to either one of these great guardians, the water would either freeze completely, or boil irrevocably. The water that supplies the plants, the creatures, and the people of Athia would vanish, and so would all that live here. So as you can see, there is more to the tale than the rhyme you are told as a child.'

Solis stopped talking and studied Soria's expression. It was unnerving. The story was meant to be just that, a story to cheer her up. Instead, she realised something. She realised that her ramblings had set something in motion. Anyone else would have been scared, as that is what Solis did best; scare the young. But Soria was different. Her sobbing had made Solis less careful about the words she had chosen. So, she tried to backtrack and make light of what she had just said. 'But it may just be a blip; who can really know these things?'

She could see the cogs turning in Soria's mind. But made peace with herself, as after all, all future leaders of Athia needed to hear the truth of the past.

As no documents were made, this task was left with Solis. She was the only one of the tribes folk who had any recollection of the past. But, this past was only passed down to the chiefs and chieftainesses. No other heard these words, as no other would have ever needed to. But Solis was now questioning her timing.

Soria stood righteously. 'So I should seek out their guardian, the white dragon? Find out what is causing this adverse weather?' She said virtuously.

Solis placed her hand on Soria's shoulder and pushed down firmly, or as firmly as an elderly lady could have. 'Sit down child. Now, is not the time to go on a quest! You are about to be coronated chieftainess of the Athianne. Maybe afterwards, much later in your life. But you cannot get across the Sapphire Stream, no person can, its suicide. The only way to find out what is happening, would be to seek advice from our guardian, the red dragon. But, such a quest would take planning and preparation. Plus, you could not do it alone. And like I said, even if you did manage to reach as far as the second mountain peak, the heat is so intense you would not survive.'

Solis, again, tried to backtrack. She realised that she had not only put the thought into Soria's mind, but she had also given her just cause and mapped out her journey. But it was already too late. She could see her mind had wandered from her words, and she was already readying herself to scale the mountain. 'I can see your mind at work. Let us get through the week and see if the heat subsides before you go running off. There are less dangerous ways to prove yourself. Saying hello to the villagers for instance and exchanging pleasantries would be a good starting point for you. Promise me, promise me, that you won't do anything stupid.'

Soria snapped out of her trance to answer. 'Of course, I promise.'

'Good, because your parents would not be best pleased with me if you went and got yourself killed before your time.'

Soria stared across the plains of Athia and looked towards the mountain peaks as she spoke. 'I promise, I won't go anywhere. Like you said, it is probably just a blip, as we are no doubt long overdue a slight weather change.'

It had been a few days since Solis saw Soria sat on that old tree stump. She regretted her poor choice in words, but blamed the heat for her slip of the tongue. Fortunately, she had not done anything so drastic as to adventure up to the top of the mountains peaks, nor had she done anything peculiar of any kind; which was highly peculiar. And, Soria had even begun to exchange pleasantries with the tribes folk. However, she knew that it would only be a matter of time before she attempted something so outlandish and hazardous. It was in her nature to seek out danger.

Chapter Seven

G lacia had been the same for a week. The heat had not risen, nor had it waned. It was the heat that had seen the Glacianne people relieve themselves of their coats and alter their clothing. Although still mightily cold, the people had begun to knit new wear. Never before had a Glacianne shown skin outside their home, other than their face and hands. The drastic weather had forced the people to shorten their attire, to something that resembled skirts and shorts on their lower half and shortened sleeves on their upper half. The night-time was still as cold as it had always been, for now, and puddles instantly froze, and from the dripping branches of fern trees formed stalactites. Then, as the sun slowly rose from the earth to the sky, the ice and snow once again became wetter and slushier.

This also called for a new tradition. Always, had the new chief/chieftainess warn a ceremonial gown upon their coronation. But the gown was designed to weather the fierce frosty temperatures during the long-winded ceremony that was about to take place.

Luckily, Nyssa, Ohmiya's mother and chieftainess of the Glacianne people, was well versed with the art of sewing and stitching. She had taken the original gown and copied its patterns to forge a new one.

She called her in from her room to see after she had finished. 'What do you think?' She said, gesturing to the magnificent piece of clothing that lay draped across the sitting room table.

It was a royal red, as it was one of the only colours, aside from green that was used in the clothing of the Glacianne people; which were usually the same darkened brown colour of mammoth skin. A large pattern had been stitched into the back. It was the shape of a snowflake. It was a mark of the people of Glacia, but also in recognition of her companion. Nyssa, who was less concerned with Snowflake as a companion, believed in her daughter entirely. She was, as well as reckless, free-spirited, and outlandish, also, kind of heart, a friend to all and always prepared to do the right thing. It was these qualities that she saw, that made her ready to lead the people into a new era.

'I absolutely love it.' Ohmiya hugged her mum and spoke softly in her ear. 'It's perfect.'

Nyssa, picked it up from the table and wrapped it around her daughter, then tied a neat, but tight, bow around the top by her neck. 'I'm so proud of you.' She said as she welled up with pride. 'You will make a fine chieftainess.'

'I hope so.' Replied Ohmiya. 'I just want to do you and father proud. And, I want to be a good leader to the Glacianne people.'

Ohmiya was thinking about what her and her father had discussed only a week before. She was thinking about how she was to deal with the threat to their land and the change in the weather. But she did not let it show. Not on that day. Not on the day when she was to become the leader of the people. She could not show any sign of weakness. So she just gave her mother a reserved smile, and went back into her room to prepare for her parents to pass the mantel later that day.

***

On the other side of the Sapphire Stream, Soria was in a state of despair. The heat ravaged the lands of Athia and had begun to claim victims. Just like Ohmiya was preparing for her ceremony, Soria's day of ascension to chieftainess had crept up on her. But, the time was not a good one, nor joyous. However, unlike usual, it was not of Soria's doing.

The heat had risen incomprehensibly and some of the elder tribe members were struggling to cope. Even Soria's father, the chief himself, was weakened by the weather. So, there was to be no ceremony and there was to be no new chief as yet. Solis was by far the worst to suffer. And, although the chief and chieftainess of Athia were feeling weakened, their only concern was for Solis.

Soria and her father and mother had visited her in her home. She was barely dressed and just modestly covered. Sweat was evaporating from her forehead as fast as it left her skin. She was gasping for every breath and struggling to speak with anyone who accompanied her bedside.

That was, until Soria entered her room. She called her over, and her mother and father joined her. Solis quickly asked if she could have a word alone with their child. The chief was not one to refuse a request from Solis, nor the chieftainess. But they were curious to hear what she wished to discuss with their daughter.

'I just wish to give the future leader a few words of wisdom, a few words of encouragement, as I have done everyone else before their time to lead. It will only take a moment.' She coughed harshly into her sheets as she spoke. 'Please, I may not get another chance.'

The chief and chieftainess bowed their heads low and left the tent, leaving only Soria and Solis in the room.

'I have to be quick.' She said. 'My time may be cut short, and I wish for you to hear what I have to say.'

'I'm listening Solis.' She replied with tears filling her eyes. She knelt next to her and put her head close to hers, so she would not have to speak louder than was necessary.

'Do you remember what I told you, only a short while ago. About the balance of life? About the Sapphire Stream?' Soria nodded, then Solis continued to speak. 'Good. It is not a tale, I mean, everything I speak is a tale. But I never made any of them up. All are true. You see, I am an old lady. Older than you might think. When I was a child, and it was my turn to receive a companion of my own. Like you I was excited, and like you I was disappointed. You see, the guardian did not bestow upon me a companion at all. I left the mountain that day heartbroken. I thought that I was not worthy of his love, so I thought I was not worthy of having a companion to look after, and to look after me.

'But this was far from the truth. He blessed me you see, with something far greater than any companion I could have hoped for. He blessed me, with some of his own life force. But, what he also blessed me with, was knowledge. I did not know it yet, as I was still so young. And that knowledge had not yet been given. You see my child, that day was over twelve hundred years ago.'

Soria stumbled in shock. 'What are you talking about? Don't be ridiculous. You cannot be that old, it's not possible.'

Soria looked deeply into the honest eyes of Solis, and she knew that what she was saying was the truth. 'But, how, why?'

Solis smiled a warming smile. 'The red dragon knew that there needed to be someone around to tell people of times gone by. That there needed to be someone to pass on our knowledge, our history. Just in case a time of need should arise. A time like now.

'I knew from the day you were born there was something special about you. I also knew from the day you were born, that something was going to happen soon after. Something that would mean that I was needed greatly, and then I would be no longer needed.'

Soria looked deeply concerned and upset, but she did not break Solis from her speech.

'I knew that it was my duty to pass down all that I knew about our history, but I knew I could not tell a child everything so directly. You seemed such a fan of all the stories that were being told by the older children, that I threw a few in there of my own. I knew that the more detail the better. You will remember the stories I speak of. I made sure that you knew all you needed to know over the years, until one day you would need to do something with that knowledge. I watched you with admiration. Your strength and self-assuredness was going to be greatly needed one day. When the people would face a time of crisis, they would need a strong leader, in whichever form that may take. I always feared the future, but I grew less nervous of it with every passing moment watching you. Now, I fear, as my time is coming to an end, that it is the start of a great and perilous journey for you. I am sorry to burden you with such a thing little one, and you may at first resent it, resent me, as I did the red dragon all those years ago. But, I am sure, you will eventually realise, that it is also a great gift. The fate of our world rests on your capable shoulders. And, it is in good hands, of that I am certain.

'But, I do not like saying goodbye, and I fear that I will not be able to hold back my feelings if we do drag this out any longer. So please, leave me with your parents, think hard of what I have said, and do not come back here. I will only grow worse, and I will not allow for you to see me when I cannot speak anymore to tell you to go.'

Soria stood up and walked to the door. She did not wish to leave Solis in such a way; not only did she have hundreds of questions that remained unanswered, she could not bear the thought of not seeing her only friend again. She stopped at the door, she did not speak, but she ran back to Solis, gave her a tight squeeze, then ran out of the tent crying uncontrollably.

Soria's mother and father did not try and stop her, and simply stepped aside before entering the tent themselves.

Soria had been sobbing for several hours. Her father walked through the door with his head bent low. Her mother had not returned and was still at the tent of Solis.

She tried to burst passed her father, but he grabbed her arm and did not let her leave. 'Let go!' She yelled at him. 'I have to see her again!'

Her father pulled her back and stood her Infront of him. Although weaker than usual, he was still impossibly strong. 'You can't daughter.' He spoke in a low tone.

'What do you mean I can't!' She replied. 'You can't stop me!'

'You are right daughter; I cannot stop you leaving the tent and going to Solis' home. Alas, she is no longer there.'

'What do you mean? She couldn't have left, not in her state.' She spoke brashly.

'No, she is still where you left her, but she is no longer with us.' Her father replied.

Soria hit the floor with a thud. Her knees instantly bruised from the impact and she couldn't stop her crying. Her father placed his hand on her back. 'I'm so sorry.' He said earnestly. 'She meant a lot to everyone. I know she meant a lot to you. And, I know how much you meant to her. But, she was old. And, now she has gone to a better place. At least you got to say goodbye. You have her last words to remember her by. Treasure them, and the memory of her will live on.' Her father did not normally do sentiment. But, the sight of his daughter tamed the angry looking giant.

Soria stopped sobbing. She thought about what Solis had said to her before her passing. Something began to ignite within her. She, somehow, knew what she had to do. As though a force unbeknown to herself compelled her to stop crying. She smiled a shallow smile.

'That's better.' Said her father. 'That's more like it. Remember the good things that Solis brought into our lives. The bad have no place in the memory of those that we have lost.'

'You are right father. She was special. I know what I have to do to honour her memory. I know what has to be done to honour her last words to me. Thanks father.'

Soria stepped into her room. She never came out for the rest of the day, and her parents dared not disturb their grieving child. Then, at nightfall she emerged. A small bag on her back that was only big enough for a small leather drinking water vessel, and a handful of herbs and roots for food. She crept like a creature of the night and left without a word, leaving the village, and headed for the mountains.

***

The Glacianne tribe had all gathered by the memorial markers in the centre of the city. They were all waiting in eager anticipation of their new chieftainess's arrival. Not a face was sad. Even though the world as they knew it was changing, and even though there was a smattering of fear spread amongst the tribes folk, they all loved and respected Ohmiya.

At the head of the crowd and stood by the great ice slabs, were Ohmiya's parents, standing proud and awaiting their beloved daughters arrival. They watched with pride as she arrived, then smiled and waved at all those that had come to greet her. At the end of the crowd of people, just before she reached her parents, was Freya. She was smiling, which was seldom seen on such a serious face. She, too, stood proud; proud to pledge her loyalty to such a fine young lady, and a fine young lady she had become.

As was tradition, before she assumed her place as chieftainess of the Glacianne people, she was to be presented with a gift; a dagger that had been passed down through the ages. It was always given to a trustworthy person within the tribe before the ceremony - a friend of the chief's and/or chieftainess' family - for them to present it to the next in line upon their coronation. This was indeed a great honour. And this time, that honour had been given to Freya.

She bent low as a mark of her allegiance before Ohmiya, and lifted a dagger above her head to be taken by the Glacianne tribe's new leader. There was no crown, and no jewels to be warn, just a dagger to be holstered by her side. It was carefully crafted by one of the first of the Glacianne leaders. It was carved from the permafrost that sits at the very end of the land of Glacia, the same ice that the memorial ice slabs are made from. It was said to be an indestructible, everlasting material, that only the flame of the red dragon could melt. Its longevity was said to represent a long and healthy leadership. It truly was an honour to be presented with such a fine piece of weaponry. And, it truly was an honour amongst the Glacianne tribes folk, to be the one chosen to present it.

Freya spoke the words that had been spoken to all those who had presented the dagger before her. 'I offer you this dagger, as a sign of the people's trust, devotion, and faith in you as our leader. May your time as our leader be as strong and as sturdy, as the very material from which it is made. Upon receiving this gift, you accept your responsibility to the people, and endeavour to do what must be done, to ensure the survival of our home and our way of life.'

Ohmiya, who only had a few words to say, had practiced for many an hour before today. Even so, she still hesitated. But only for a moment. Then she recited the vow that had been spoken so many times before her. 'I take this dagger, and in receipt of this honour I pledge myself, and all that I am, to the people of Glacia.'

Ohmiya lifted the permafrost dagger from Freya. She stroked the intricate pattern that was carved into the blade. It was, as it obviously would have been, cold to the touch, which is why it was given a leather handle. The mammoth skin handle kept the cold within and made it easier to grasp. She placed it in its holster, and with that,

Freya rose. All that was left of the ceremony was for her mother and father to relinquish the right to rule in front of the rest of the tribe and appoint a successor.

She walked hesitantly, nervously, towards her parents. She smiled to disguise the stress she was under. Her parents beamed with pride as she approached them. Freya took her place next to the chief and chieftainess, placed her arms firmly by her sides and watched over the crowd. As the one to hand over the dagger, she was also the one to be advisor to their successor.

'Well, daughter, are you ready?' Said Ohmiya's father.

She took a deep breath. 'I am ready father.'

He turned to the people, and without the need for any voice enhancer, his voice echoed through the city. 'Today!' He bellowed. 'Today, in light of our current situation; today is a joyous day! Today is a wondrous day!' Everyone began to cheer loudly.

The scales of the dragon skin that formed the walls of the city had begun to shake. The cheers and chants became louder, and the shaking of the large diamond scales became worse. The chief continued his speech and remained unaware. However, Freya was all too aware of what was happening. She tried to get the chief to tone down his speech.

'Nonsense.' He said. 'I want the world to hear what I have to say! Because today! Today is the day that, I, the chief of the Glacianne people. Today is the day, that I retire my position, and appoint

Ohmiya, my daughter the new...' He spoke with excitement and was blissfully ignorant to the scales falling from the walls and the ceiling. The dragons skin that had kept the people of Glacia safe had begun to fall. A large scale from the ceiling cracked, then broke away. The sun shone radiantly through the crack and into the chief's eyes. He shielded his face and stopped talking. Then, there was a mad panic. Everyone had suddenly become aware of what was happening and started to run for cover. Houses fell under the rock-solid scales. Like large, razor-sharp panes of glass, they caused mass destruction. The chief was in shock, watching over as his people were crushed under the walls that were supposed to protect them, powerless to help them.

He was paralyzed to the spot for a moment. Until, he heard an almighty crack from above. A large piece of the ceiling had broken away. It was falling at speed. He had no time to think, as it was heading straight for Ohmiya, who was also paralyzed with fear. He dived through the air and pushed her out of the way. She was lifted from her feet and flew several metres away from where she was standing. She rose, no longer frozen, and looked over to where she was previously stood. Her father had pushed her to safety, but in doing so, had been hit by the large scale that had targeted her. He had been crushed under the weight of it. Her mother was trying desperately to lift it to free him. Freya, too, tried to help. Then, another member of the tribe, then another. It took six people to lift the scale from off of her father.

All were in disarray, and no one, not even Ohmiya, knew what to say. It was obvious to all that he was no longer alive; his lifeless body lay limp in the slushy snow. She fell to the floor and placed her arms over him, crying.

The scales stopped falling and the rest of the Glacianne gathered around them, except those who were seeing to a fallen member of their own family. She did not let go of her father; she did not stop crying. Everyone got down on their knees and began to whisper words of prayer.

'Come on young one.' Said Freya. And, she grabbed Ohmiya by the arm and lifted her to her feet. It took a few tugs, as she would not let go of her father willingly. 'Come on Ohmiya, this will not do you any good. Lift yourself from the ground. He is gone. There is nothing that can be done. All that can be done now, is for you to stand. All that can be done to honour your father now, is to rise up and become what you were meant to be, to become the leader that the Glacianne people need you to be right now.'

Ohmiya, still broken, stumbled to her feet with the help of Freya. She looked desperately at her father on the floor. She could not process what had just happened, as it all seemed to happen so quickly. She only knew to listen to her advisor. She only knew that she was now the leader of the people. If her father had taught her anything, it was that life will throw things at her that would be unexpected, and sometimes they would be inexplicably difficult. But as a leader, you must remain resolute and strong in the face of those you are tasked to lead. Then, when you are alone, or in trusted company, only then you can show emotion. So, she knew that this was one of those moments. This was a time to be strong. Later she would allow herself to feel. Later she would reveal, in her own company, the pain she was now feeling.

She spoke loud and clear for all to hear. 'I, Ohmiya, newly appointed chieftainess of the Glacianne people, will vow to resolve our current crisis. I, like the rest of you, am scared. But, I will not let that fear stand in my way. It has been obvious for weeks now, that something is happening to Glacia. The broken walls of our city is proof enough, that this matter is to be taken more seriously than was first thought. In honour of my father, I will not rest until the Glacianne people can once again feel safe in their homes. I will make sure that I lead us all into a better future. This I vow to you, today, as my first act as chieftainess of this fine tribe.'

There was silence for a moment, then a raw of cheer from the crowd. Then, Ohmiya, along with her mother and Freya, carried her father away and back to their home. Everyone parted for the fallen former chief and remained quiet in a mark of respect. Ohmiya did not know where the strength had come from to give such a powerful speech, or indeed, how she was going to live up to such a promise. She had singlehandedly guaranteed her tribes safety and wellbeing, without a thought as to how she was to achieve this. One thing was certain though, she was never the same again after that day.

The night had fallen over a saddened Glacia. The air was damp, as damp as the floor. Snow was melting at an astounding rate, and the people had made their way out of the city. Makeshift tents were erected fairly quickly and the tribe had begun to take it in turns to retrieve resources needed from their homes and the storage facilities. Only food, clothing and weapons were permitted to be collected.

The children and injured, were the only ones that were exempt from entering the cities walls. The fit and able, men and women alike, were made to collect. The only Glacianne that remained in the city, were Ohmiya, Freya, and Nyssa.

They were in Ohmiya's sitting room. None had spoken for twenty minutes. Non knew what the other one was thinking.

Nyssa was grieving, and her thoughts were occupied with worry for her daughter. She had been given the title of chieftainess, lost her father, and was about to lose her home, all in that very same day.

Freya was looking at Ohmiya intently. She was trying to ascertain her thoughts. But, she was a closed book. Expressionless and motionless, she sat in her father's armchair in the living room. She was buried in the crevice that had formed under the enormity of her father's weight as he had sat there.

Ohmiya was deep in thought. She was not grieving, nor had she yet accepted her father's fate. She was focused. She had just stood before her people and vowed to end the crisis they were currently facing. But, as her father was not there to guide her through it, and she did not wish to bother her mother at that time, she remained focused on the last conversation she had had with him. Every word he uttered was now etched into her memory.

'Well, in the event that our walls begin to crumble. It is my duty as chief of this tribe to find out what is causing the problem. So, I will scale the mountain with my companion while our people are still safe behind these walls. I will go up to the cave where the white dragon lays slumber and I will find out what to do from there.' Were the words that her father had said to her. So, now it was her duty to make that very same journey.

She rose from the seat. 'I must pack immediately. I must go tonight.' She said.

Freya stayed silent. But, Nyssa finally broke from her trance. 'What are you talking about child? You are not going anywhere. The Glacianne people need you.'

'That, mother, is precisely why I must leave. The answers we seek are not here, they are up the mountain, with the white dragon. It is there I must go, to seek council from him. Only he can tell us how to resolve this problem.'

'You sit back down young lady. You are to pack only what we need like the rest of us, and stay here with me to help the tribe fix this catastrophe. You leaving now would seem as though you have abandoned your people. Tell her Freya. Advise her on what to do.'

Freya looked at Ohmiya, then turned to Nyssa. 'I'm afraid.' She paused, sighed, then continued. 'I'm afraid she is right, Nyssa.'

Nyssa looked at Freya Crossly and pointed her finger jaggedly in her face. 'You will listen to your leader, as chieftainess of this tribe...'

Freya interjected sternly. 'If I may! That is exactly what I am doing. And, with all due respect, Nyssa, it is Ohmiya who is now the chieftainess of the Glacianne people.' Freya turned to Ohmiya and smiled. 'You have become quite the young woman, Ohmiya. You have come a long way from that tearaway child that I once knew. If you feel that the best possible chance the people have of getting through this is to go seek guidance from our guardian, then I will gladly follow you and protect you on your mission.

Ohmiya smiled back at Freya. 'No.' She said bluntly. 'I will not be needing anyone to accompany me. It is my duty as chieftainess to do this alone. I will not risk the lives of my people by taking away their best line of defence.'

Freya seemed taken back by the decline for her assistance. ' But, Ohmiya, I must insist. You will surely die if you made such a journey alone. Who would protect you? Snowflake, I dare say, is of no use against the monsters that live beyond our borders. Once you leave the gates that guard the Glacianne tribe, you are all but defenceless. Who will lead us if you don't return? This would not be what your father would want.'

'I appreciate your concern and loyalty to my family, Freya. But what use is a leader if there is no one left to lead? With our cities walls falling, and our lands around the gates melting, it may only be a matter of time before the creatures that lurk outside become curious. What if they breach the gates. We no longer have the protection of our cities walls. I need you here with the people. If we are attacked, then I need you to lead the rest of the hunters against any potential invasion. And, I think it is exactly what my father would want. When we last spoke, he was planning to make this journey himself. He did not talk of a convoy, or even a guard for protection. He said, that it was his duty as chief to do it alone. So, it is now my duty. And, I will not make my first act as chieftainess of this tribe, be to neglect the words of their former leader. My mind is made.'

Nyssa, still in disbelief, was unsure of what to say. 'I don't believe what I am hearing.' She said. 'I am not sure how I should be feeling.'

'Proud.' Replied Freya. 'I would feel proud. I am proud, to serve such a remarkable young woman. You pack what you need young one. I will see to it that your mother and I are ready to leave this home.'

Nyssa, still unsure how she was feeling, was guided by Freya to the kitchen. 'Grab as much as you can carry.' She said softly. 'Food and water only would be my advice.'

Ohmiya, still unsure how she was feeling, looked down at Snowflake. He looked up at her with wide eyes and a wide toothless smile. The same look that he had given her upon their first meeting. He was either blissfully unaware of the feat they now faced, or willing to walk into fire alongside her. It did not matter. She knew that with Snowflake by her side she was never going to be alone. 'Come on then. Let us pack. We have a long journey ahead of us.'

She left her home with her mother and Freya. There hadn't been a word spoken since Ohmiya made her decision against her mother's advice. But after they left out the door, Nyssa spoke plainly to her daughter. 'You don't have to do this you know. We can find another way, together. Please, just sleep on it tonight. You can go tomorrow if you still feel the same.'

'I can't.' She replied. 'This is something I must do. I promise, I will come home.'

Nyssa hugged her daughter tightly. 'You had better.' She said. 'I can't cope with losing you too. I don't think I could bear it.'

'I promise I'll come home to you. You won't lose me too.' Ohmiya knew that her promise was one she could not guarantee she could keep. But, she could not tell her mother how she truly felt.

The journey ahead of her was one that had not ever been done. So, there was no way to guarantee her safe return. She began to tear again, so she quickly let go of her mother and headed in the opposite direction.

She snuck through one of the cracks that was made in the cities walls, and left out of the gate when no one was watching. Stealth was one thing that Ohmiya never lacked. She had been forever wandering off in her youth, making the adults worry about her whereabouts; only to return several hours later unharmed. This stealth was something she would rely on greatly, if she was to make it up the mountain alive. But, she also packed the ceremonial dagger. She feared to use such a weapon, as she was averse to violence and any form it took. But she was not averse to remaining alive, and needed to keep something with her as a means of protection. Because, as had been pointed out to her frequently, Snowflake was as useful as a protector, as a wooden raft would be for crossing the Sapphire Stream.

Chapter Eight

Soria had wandered for several hours. She remembered the journey to the mountain peaks well, the same journey she had made twelve years before. Although, due to the intense increase in heat, she did not remember it taking so long. She was much older and much stronger than she was at five years old, and she was equally determined to make the trip; maybe even more so than when she was only a youngling. But, the closer she got to the mountains, the hotter the air became. The airless warmth stole her strength; the harder she pushed on, it seemed as though an equal force pushed her back. Mr. Fuzzy, who seemed completely unaffected by the weather, trotted along happily next to her.

Etherflame blazed brightly as the midday came, as the heat had caused some to spontaneously ignite. Soria plucked some from the ground that had not yet flamed. They had a great many uses. They could be crushed and eaten alone or with other foods. The Athianne had done this for many years, until other delectable treats began to grow. It is said, the Athianne's resilience to heat was partly to do with diet, as well as where they were born. The properties of the Etherflame would supposedly allow the one who consumed them to withstand higher than normal temperatures. However, this theory had never actually been tested. But Soria knew of this, as it was one of the many hints and tips hidden amongst Solis' stories. So she packed a couple, along with a handful of sticks, into her tiny bag. The Etherflame were also useful as a torch at night. She was only sure of one thing; that she would need all the help that she could get, and the land was full of helpful items. But she was unable to carry anything more.

Soria had spent many years with her own company. Never once, though, had she reflected on times gone by. Always had she thought ahead. However, now she was thinking, and thinking hard at past decisions. If her way of being was truly all bad, then why would Solis have told her what she did? Was it necessary? Was she purposefully born a solitary creature? Was she hardened by the will of the guardian that the Athianne serve, as it was someone who needed to be strong to carry out such a task, such a journey?

Reflection of self would usually have occurred when one had an epiphany, and surrenders their former self to the past, making way for a new improved version. Soria, though, did not feel the need to surrender who she once was entirely, as Solis' words made her believe that there was nothing wrong with the person she was. She had almost succumbed to the notion that she needed to change. She had all but decided to change her nature completely upon her last talk with Aylen. The once timid little girl, that feared the very thought of Soria, was now one to be feared. So, she realised a complete change was unnecessary. She had watched as Aylen had alienated herself; with an increase in strength and in confidence, had also spawned an ignorance within her. She was once friend to all, yet had become friendly towards none. You see, what Aylen had failed to realise, is that her hatred for Soria, and her need to be better than she was had had the opposite effect. She had become her nemesis rather than become better than her.

Soria was indeed a tough person, a hard person. But she was observant, intelligent and wise beyond her years. She realised, during her lonely walk in the heat, she was not in need of a complete transformation, and that she was in need of a makeover. The qualities she possessed were required. But to succeed in life, to succeed as a leader, she needed to be more than just tough. A balance of strength and benevolence would be needed; tipping the scales too far either way would lose her the people. This journey alone would require the strength of a hundred leaders. Yet, upon her return she would not allow herself to be smug. Upon her return, she would demonstrate to the people that she sacrificed herself, not as a means of proving something to herself, but to prove to the people that she was worthy of their love and of their loyalty. That was of course, if she was successful in her quest and if she was to return at all.

This would be hard for Soria, as it was in her nature to be ruthless. To be feared was something she fed on. Being tough was written in her DNA, and it pained her to exchange pleasantries to the villagers only the week before.

She watched the other animals as she wandered. The crimson coated fox of Athia, was not a solitary creature like a regular fox. In fact, most of the creatures of Athia ran together in packs. She watched as they came up close to her, close enough to touch. She reached out a hand and one allowed her to stroke its fur. She did so and smiled. She reached out for another fox. It was not so easily swayed and moved away. The first fox then moved back towards her. It allowed for Soria to stroke it instead of the other.

She watched this behaviour and thought deeply about why they did this. It didn't make sense to her at first, so she thought nothing more of it. Although she could practice kindness on the creatures of

Athia, she needed human contact to learn from. As Soria, now, wished to learn how to be better than she was; she wished to learn about compassion and love for another, other than herself. And, although she would never admit it, her love for Mr. Fuzzy.

***

A deep crunching and cracking sound resonated up ahead. The smell of death drifted down the mountain. The snow was stained freshly red and Ohmiya's boot squelched as she stepped through it. It was not the well-known squelching sound that was made from her boots, but a mixture of blood, surface water and slush.

Ohmiya, being Ohmiya, was drawn to find the source. She followed the trail cautiously up the mountain. It was not long before she saw it. A half alive, Glacianne ox. It was a large creature. It donned a sparkly white fur coat, with huge antlers. They were not regular antlers, nor could it be presumed that they were made of bone. If one did not know they were there, one might have assumed it had none, as they were crystal clear; like glass sculptures attached to its head, and practically invisible against the powdered snow.

It was an extremely large, strong animal. Whoever, or whatever had taken it down, must have been incredibly strong also. But, at the time, Ohmiya was not concerned with what had brought down the beast, and more concerned with helping it. You see, Ohmiya found it hard to accept that she was consuming another creature when eating, and was completely averse to the idea of killing. But, as there were very few edible greens in Glacia, she was forced to eat, or starve.

She took a step closer to the ox with caution. It groaned a sorrowful grown and snorted sickly. It was nearing its end, that much was certain, and there was nothing that could be done but comfort the creature. She was now close enough to reach out and touch it. At first, it thrashed its head and waved its mighty antlers in her direction. She pulled back her hand and stepped back quickly. That was its last effort, as its energy had all but diminished. Although she knew that it could no longer move, one swing of its antlers would undoubtedly result in Ohmiya's death. So, her movements remained sloth like.

She reached out again. It did not move. She placed her hand on its chest. It was warm, warmer than she would have expected. There was life left in it. It was a stubborn creature that was clinging on to every second it could.

She looked to its rear. A large gaping wound was still seeping lifeblood. Ohmiya was distraught. She turned to Snowflake for advice, knowing it was a pointless exercise. He too looked sad. He had never witnessed such a thing and his usual gormless grin was nowhere to be seen.

'What should I do?' Ohmiya asked.

Snowflake shrugged his whole body, so she assumed he had understood what she was asking. Although, no one had ever been certain that Snowflake understood anything. This was the first time he had ever done anything, other than smile excessively and snuggle with those who would offer him a cuddle. Other than that, he was Ohmiya's shadow. Only, at that moment in time, it would seem he possessed more emotions than one had first thought possible.

'I don't know either.' Replied Ohmiya to her own question.

She realised that the journey she was on was going to be far longer than she first thought, with only Snowflake for company, as she was going to have to form both parts of the conversation.

The ox groaned loudly. It was clearly in a lot of pain. She knew what she had to do to put it out of its misery, but she did not feel as though she had the strength. She looked at Snowflake one more time, hoping he might offer an alternative solution. But he just looked up at her sadly.

She dropped her bag to the floor and drew out the dagger. Her left hand was shaking, so she placed it in her right. Her right hand had begun to shake, so she held her forearm tightly with her free left hand. She held it out of sight of the ox, as she did not want to startle it any further.

She hesitated, and the ox groaned again loudly. Ohmiya began to cry silently. Tears on her face, that would normally have crystallised in the cold, splashed in the slush.

'I can't do it.' She said to herself. 'I just can't do it.'

The earth began to tremble, the air again smelt of death. Something was coming. It was large, it was very large. Trees began to fall in the distance, and something was ploughing its way through. The ox groaned and looked longingly into Ohmiya's bright blue eyes. It was pleading to her without words, to do what she had said she could not.

The ox knew that if she did not, it would meet a grisly end at the hands of whatever was coming. The earth shook harder, and the deathly smell grew stronger. It was unmistakably the breath of a yeti. Ohmiya would never have forgotten it. That very same stench she smelt the first time she climbed the mountain as a youngling. They were horrible, vicious creatures. It would no doubt have enjoyed devouring the ox alive, taking pleasure in it even.

Ohmiya looked back at the ox; she understood what it wanted. She drew the knife so it could see. It did not swing for her, and it turned away. It laid there and waited for her to do what had to be done, so the ox could die as quickly and painlessly as possible.

The yeti was too close for comfort. It was practically on top of them. She placed her hand on the cheek of the ox and stroked its fur one last time. Floods of tears fell down her face. With one strong, stabbing motion, she plunged the dagger hard and deep into its chest. The ox was almost instantly dead.

Snowflake could see that she was frozen to the spot. She was in shock at what she had just done, as this was the first life that she had taken. But there was no time to sit around. The yeti was almost there, so Snowflake tugged at her skirt with his mouth. She pulled herself together and ran for the nearest source of cover. She lifted a fallen fern tree branch and covered both her and Snowflake with it.

She peered through the thin spindly branches and watched as the yeti appeared. She was horrified as it let out an almighty raw, beat its chest and stamped its feet like a gorilla. It was angry, very angry. Yetis were vile and liked their food alive. Ohmiya had denied this brute that pleasure, and gave the ox a more honourable death. It had obviously wounded it, left it there to suffer, before returning later to finish the job.

She watched in horror as the yeti lifted the poor ox into the air, and pulled it apart. Ohmiya could not look anymore, as it was too horrible to witness. So she closed her eyes, and tried desperately to think of home, and of nice, warming thoughts.

It had only been a few minutes, although to Ohmiya, it felt like hours. The yeti had finished its meal and was deeply unsatisfied. It stamped and rampaged for another minute, until it finally calmed down. Snowflake was tucked tightly under Ohmiya's body and they both stayed impossibly quiet. The yeti may have had an atrocious smelling breath, but they had next to no sense of smell. They relied solely on sight and hearing. One wrong movement, and both Ohmiya and Snowflake could have met the same atrocious end.

The yeti gave one last sweep of the area and made its way back down the mountain. Ohmiya was thankful, as this meant he was going in the opposite direction. Yet it was not the only one, nor the biggest, or the fiercest. Stories had been told as warnings to the younglings, so they would not venture out of the confines of the Glacianne city. The larger more vicious creatures lived up the mountain, or so the stories went, so by all accounts, eluding this one was a walk in the park. The others would not be so easily avoided.

Ohmiya was well aware of the potential dangers that were ahead, but this event did not sway her from her mission. Should the cities walls fall, the Glacianne, her people, would be exposed to dangers such as this on a daily basis. And, the yeti were only one of many carnivorous beasts in Glacia.

She lifted the leaves from off of her head and threw the branch to one side. The blade was wiped on the end of her skirt, which stained it slightly a softened pink. Ohmiya lifted Snowflake onto her shoulder and pushed him against her cheek. She felt more protective over her companion from then. He was going to be her source of strength, even though he possessed none physically, she knew she could not make the journey to the white dragon without his help.

'Well, we best get going Snowflake. No more detours, I promise. We hear anything else, no matter how horrifying it might be, we keep moving. Because if I don't do this, our people, our family, may share that ox's fate. And I cannot let that happen.'

Chapter Nine

S oria had scaled the mountainous terrain with her companion for most of the day. The sun had fallen and no longer gave enough light to allow them to proceed. They needed to look for somewhere to spend the night. The Athianne sky never offered a drop of rain, nor did it host any clouds. The sky was an oil painting; a deep, deep blue smudged with pinks and purples. And, with no likely attack from any creature, there was no need for shelter. But, as it was human nature to seek out cover for the night, she did so.

They had reached the top of the first mountain peak. Each step she had taken to the top had made for an unpleasant memory. She remembered racing to the top. She remembered her arrogance. She remembered the yearning she felt, as though she had to make it to the top quickly in fear of something bad happening. Then she remembered, as she looked upon the entrance to the cave, the dragons carved into the wall that stared hollowly at her, and the disappointment she felt as her companion came forth from darkness and into the light.

She stood upon the mountain top and stared out over Athia, her land. The fading light of the sun had hidden behind the third mountain peak and succumbed to the night. The land below was alive with the light of the Etherflame that burned bright in the night. As she looked out over the vast lands, the flames burned like city lights in a display most magnificent. The breeze swayed lightly back and forth from the cavern entrance, like the mountain itself breathed life into the land. The sweet scent of the burning lands drifted up the mountain, and as Soria drew breath herself, she smiled unwittingly as she exhaled. Never had anyone in her lifetime observed such a sight. She felt a warmth from within, which lightened her mood, stole away from her the past memories that haunted her, and made way for a fresh new one.

She tilted her head toward her shoulder, where Mr. Fuzzy perched himself like a pirate's parrot. 'What do you think?' She asked him.

Mr. Fuzzy yawned widely, licked her face with his large wet tongue and pressed his face firmly against her cheek. In the past she might have pushed him off her shoulder and give him a swift kick. And, although she felt an urge to do something horrible, she resisted the temptation, calmed herself down, unwrinkled her eyebrows and smiled flatly at him.

She turned away from the land below and stared into the blackness before her. The cave entrance hadn't changed one bit. It was exactly the same as she remembered it. Like an infinite void of nothingness was staring at her. Her eyes went funny and began losing focus, so she looked away.

The only shelter for miles was the cavern itself, but it looked safer on the outside. She dared not take a step closer. Mr. Fuzzy hopped off of her shoulder and made his way to the entrance obliviously.

'Come back you stupid furball!' she cried. 'We will have to look for another way to the top.'

He stopped, turned and stared blankly back at her. She gave a sigh of relief. 'Thank you. Now, come back here.' She said. 'We will figure out what to do in the morning.'

The side of the mountain was an uninviting, harsh, rocky surface. Setting up camp was going to be tricky. Sleeping too close to the edge of the mountain top was suicide, as she may have rolled over the edge in her sleep, and she was not willing to sleep too near to the cavern entrance. She knew deep down that there was nothing to fear, but she feared it anyway. So, their only option was to make cosy by the rough rocky surface in the centre. Luckily for Soria, she had spent many nights laid under the stars, so it was not something that concerned her.

When she was only a youngling, many times had Solis carried her in from the outskirts of the village and placed her in her own bed. She often fell asleep against a nearby rock, or large stone under the stars. She looked up at them, the stars, and wondered if Solis was out there. She wondered if she was looking down on her. She began to well-up at the thought of her late friend, as she was the only real friend she had ever had. But Solis told Soria many stories, and some of them were of the stars and how they came to be.

One of the stories went, that all stars are souls of those who no longer are, and also, souls of those who will come to be. So, when someone passes, and they return to the heavens, they can advise those who are about to begin their own life's journey on earth. Soria liked this story, as it made the idea of death easier. Because a soul never truly dies, and it is never truly born. It always is, and always has been, and will always be. She took comfort in knowing her friend was still out there and watching over her. But, it also placed pressure on her. She wanted to make her proud, even more so than she wanted to make her parents proud. Only now, she was watching her every move from above.

Soria's mind kept whirring in thought, as she continued to gaze into the nights sky. The stars began to dance, then spin, until she had fallen into a deep dreamless sleep.

⁂

Nyssa and Freya were counting heads and making sure that everyone was accounted for. A large thunderous crack struck the air. It was not the first, nor would it be the last. With every passing hour, more and more of the dragon skin city was falling. Large scales broke away, which left large holes in the home of the Glacianne.

Everyone was frantic with fear, yet Freya tried to herd the tribe and reassure those in a state of panic. Nyssa was helping worried parents find their children and helping Freya round them all up into the same spot.

'Is that everyone?' asked Nyssa.

'I think so.' Replied Freya, who had one eye focused on the walls. The watchers had not abandoned their posts, but they were too busy focusing on what was happening inside the walls.

Freya grabbed her horn from within her coat and blew hard into it. It gained the attention of everyone, even the guards who stood in the watch towers high above. She signalled for them to avert their attention to the outside of the gates, and called for all watchers and hunters to stand to attention.

'Listen up everyone. Anyone who is not either looking for loved ones, injured, or otherwise indisposed, follow me to the gate. All towers must be guarded, and they must be guarded immediately. The towers on the east and the west are unmanned. Zorn and Ceyhan; you stand guard in the watch towers.' She ordered the two Glacianne, and they listened and followed her instruction without resistance, as Freya was deeply respected by all. Then, she continued to address the rest of the people. 'Everyone else make a perimeter within the walls. Our city has fallen, and all that stands between us and the creatures that lurk on the outskirts, are the wooden spires. The sound of our city falling will no doubt have caught their attention. They may become curious, braver, and venture closer for a look. We need to make sure that they know we are not vulnerable, and that we will still attack if they try to breach. They should not be able to get through, but we mustn't assume anything.'

Nyssa looked at Freya for advice. Freya was alone, had always been alone, and that was how she liked it. So, aside from Ohmiya, who she considered the daughter she never had, she had no one to be concerned about other than herself. Nyssa, on the other hand, had just lost her partner. The man she had been with for as long as she could remember, and thus could not remember a life without him by her side. She was all but lost, and wandering around aimlessly now that everyone was out to safety.

'Nyssa. Nyssa!' Freya called to break her from her trance.

'Are you okay? In fact don't answer that. I know you're not okay. You just go with everyone else to the centre. I will keep watch over us with the rest of the hunters and watchers. We will take it in turns to rest every few hours and we will keep doing this for as long as is necessary.'

Nyssa looked concerned. 'And, just how long will be necessary?' She asked.

Freya placed her hand on Nyssa's shoulder. 'That, I am afraid, is up to the young chieftainess of this tribe. When she returns from the mountain we will know what to do.'

Nyssa did not say anything, but Freya could see in her eyes what she was going to ask. Then, she restrained herself, as she did not wish to know the answer. But, Freya gave her an answer anyway. 'She will return Nyssa. It is a matter of when, not if. Your daughter is strong. She is strong in ways I cannot explain. I have no doubt she will be back soon.'

Nyssa gave a half smile, as though she was partially reassured, yet she could not help but fear for her daughter. She had already lost her husband and could not bear the thought of losing her daughter too. 'Thank you.' She replied. 'You are right. Of course you are, she will be back before we know it.'

Freya gave a half smile in return. 'You just go with the rest of the tribe now. Look after the people; the injured and vulnerable need you, you can do no further good here. Ohmiya may be the new chieftainess, but the tribe still looks to you for guidance. Look after your people and I will keep them safe. Go!'

On the outskirts of the Glacianne walls. Wolves had been scrambling and rising in numbers. They were approaching the gate. Watchers alerted the hunters below. They opened the gates and readied their defences. The armouries had been raided before everyone had evacuated the city, and they had extracted enough weapons to fight a small war; more than enough to warn off a ravenous pack of wolves.

The gates crashed open and a hoard of hunters stampeded like a herd of elephants out of the city. They charged at the wolves and forced them back into the forest. Then, they cautiously returned back through the gates again, safe.

Zorn shouted from the east tower. 'They shall not be gone for long! More will arrive shortly! I can see shadows gathering in the distance!' he said.

Freya shouted back. 'And we shall be ready for them when we do! We stand behind high walls for a reason, and our numbers still exceed their own. We shall not be breached. We must not allow our city to fall, not today, not ever.'

Everyone cheered her and they all went back to their posts. Freya was tough on the exterior and never doubted herself. But, that was when she only had to rely on herself. Never had she put so much trust in another. Never had she had to sit and wait. She only knew how to act, how to take charge. But, this was a fight that was being fought on two fronts. The front line with the hunters and the watchers of the Glacianne tribe, and then there was the young chieftainess in the making, Ohmiya. She was all alone in the vastness of Glacia, practically unprotected. And, the people relied on her making a journey, that had never before been made.

I hope you know what you are doing. I hope you are okay. Freya thought to herself. Then, she again took her position.

The wolves had not ventured far. They had spotted the footprints that had been made in the snow. They had picked up on the scent of the Glacianne that had made them. Ohmiya was careful, and made sure she was not seen. But, what she hadn't counted on, was her smell that remained permanently in footprints in the snow. A smell that was carried sweetly down the mountain and into the noses of the wolves at the bottom. They no longer cared for the dangerous meal that was safely guarded behind the wall. They had a new target. A tasty treat that tottered up the mountain *alone*.

***

The sun had awoken and begun to rise over Athia. The rays crept slowly around the mountain scape and stroked Soria's face. She gradually opened her eyes, she did not move at first, as she was still half asleep. She stretched out like a feline and reached beside her where Mr. Fuzzy had fallen asleep next to her. But he wasn't there.

She leapt from the ground like a startled cat and scouted the area. He was nowhere to be seen. A sudden gut-wrenching pain hit her in the pit of her stomach. Her companion was nowhere to be seen, and she was all alone atop the first peak of the Athianne mountains. Soria rarely felt fear, but at that moment, she was scared, flustered and panicking. The little creature that had often been poked, prodded and pushed away, had now become the only thing that was keeping her sane. She knew instantly that she could not make the journey without him and she looked around frantically; firstly looking down the mountain to see if he had had a tumble, secondly looking around the peak to see if he had hidden behind a bush or stone, then thirdly she looked into the entrance.

She turned away, but then she looked back sharply. It was no longer infinitely black, no longer impossible to see into. It had come alive with light. The entrance was flickering with a blood orange glow, like a torch light had been lit from within it.

How is that possible? She thought to herself. 'Where is that light coming from?' She said aloud.

She feared that something had taken Mr. Fuzzy, taken him into the caves entrance. Either that, or he had awoken before she had and followed the light into the cave.

So she ran through without a care and began to shout. 'Mr. Fuzzy! Are you there?'

No answer came back, no one spoke, and there was no noise of any kind. Then, *'Mr. Fuzzy! Are you there?'* echoed back. The walls replied to her. She had never heard an echo before, as there were no other caves in Athia, nor were there anywhere that one's voice could echo.

For a minute, she had forgotten all about her lost companion and continued to shout deep into the cave. 'Helloooo!' She shouted. And, *'Helloooo!'* Came back.

'Is anybody there?' she shouted again. And, *'Is anybody there?'* came back again.

The light in the cave grew brighter, harsher, until it looked as though it was coming for Soria. *What the hell is that?* She thought. She turned away and began to run, but it was closing in on her. The light was catching up, she had strolled so far into the cave that she was lost. The entrance was nowhere in sight and she needed the light that she was trying to escape from to see. A wall blocked her way, there was nowhere to run and nowhere to hide. 'I'm not afraid of you!' she bellowed. *'I'm not afraid of you!'* bounced back.

She stood still but was shaking a little. She positioned herself ready to fight, arms raised, fists clenched and feet spread apart. It was almost on top of her. Whatever the light was coming from, it was close. 'Show yourself coward!' she shouted without conviction.

It got closer, and closer, and closer. Then, out popped Mr. Fuzzy, waddling desperately to catch up to his keeper. He was panting and gasping for breath. His little feet had struggled to keep up with Soria's speedy sprinting.

She was relieved, but her face looked annoyed. 'Where the hell did you go?' she shouted at him. 'I was worried sick about you.' She began to cry with relief.

His face lit up and he beamed a big smile, as she whisked him from his feet and into her arms. 'Don't you ever do that to me again.' She continued to tell him off like a child that had wandered off.

It took a while for her to realise that the glow was coming from his fur. His fur flickered a blood orange, like a tiny flame with feet.

'Why are you glowing? How are you glowing?' she held him out in front of her and inspected him like she was checking him for ticks. 'Where is the light coming from? You look like a nightlight.'

He smiled the same gormless smile he always did, and panted with his tongue out like a happy puppy. She raised an eyebrow sarcastically 'Now?' she asked rhetorically. 'Now you show off an ability. After twelve years of torment, twelve years of doing nothing useful, you finally show me that you can do more than smile at me foolishly, like you have been dropped a few too many times.'

Soria studied him. 'I suppose glowing isn't much to brag about, though, is it. But, I guess we don't have to walk up the mountain now. We can just walk through the caves. Maybe one of these paths will lead to the top.'

She was about to drop him on the floor when she noticed something on the wall up ahead. She clutched a tuft of fur from behind his neck and lifted him into the air like a lantern.

She set off forward slowly, 'What's that I wonder?' she whispered rhetorically.

The walls had been marked. But these markings were unlike anything she had ever seen. They were pictures drawn in a dark coloured chalk, and the pictures seemed to tell a story. It looked familiar to a tale she had heard as a youngling. One of the older boys, Naavo, had told her a story. It was a story she remembered very well, a story she liked very much. But never before had she seen images that would enact the words. She whispered the story as she waved Mr. Fuzzy over the pictures.

'Validan, the chief of the Athianne at around one thousand years ago, was a strong and powerful leader. He rained when Athia was home to vicious creatures, who shared the land with humans. One group in particular, the lycunflame, were the most cunning and terrifying of all of these creatures. They would hunt at the dead of night, snatch the weak and the vulnerable from their tents, and carry them back up to the mountain.

'Validan, and a small group of warriors in his ranks, charged up the mountains one morning where the lycunflame lived. He was tired

of the wolf like beasts coming down the mountains at night, and attacking the Athianne. He knew he had to protect his tribe from these savage creatures, so he went to their home while they slept, just as they did to his.

'They found the lycunflame, asleep. Before they had chance to rouse they...'

Soria stopped for a minute and inspected the pictures. The story veered in a different direction. She had not seen, this, ending before. She had not seen what was being told in the chalk drawn storyboard. She was always told that they slayed the lycunflame while they slept. But, before they were able to kill them all, some of the larger ones awoke. They attacked the Athianne and slaughtered all but one; Validan was all that remained. Him and the largest of the lycunflame, the leader of the pack. He faced him in a showdown of strength and will. Validan was the victor in the story she knew. He and his warriors killed them all. But, it was only he who returned. So, it was only his story that was heard.

This story ended differently, though. It did not show a battle of brawn, a battle to the death. It showed the lycunflame asleep and the Athianne approaching them, yet it did not show either one attack the other. Instead, it showed a barrier of boulders falling from the sky. It showed them, the boulders, block everyone on one side of the cave, leaving only one on the other side, presumably Validan. Then it ended. *Is that what happened? Really? A rockslide?* She thought disappointedly.

'The great Validan, my ancestor, who was deemed some kind of great hero, was no hero. It was nothing more than dumb luck. A rockslide is what blocked the lycunflame off from the rest of Athia. The lycunflame and those poor people, were trapped on the other side, along with whatever horrors lie beyond the blockade of boulders.

Soria hadn't realised how far she had walked. The drawings had taken her to the very end of the cave. It was a dead end, with no way through and no way up the mountain. She bashed the boulders in frustration and let out a screech. It echoed through the cave and rattled the walls. 'This can't be the only way up! There has to be another way, there just has to be!'

She let out another screech in anger, which again echoed through the cave and shook the walls.

She raised Mr. Fuzzy, who was still alight, to see if she could see a way round. Then, she lifted him higher. 'What is that?' she whispered. Then she fell back in fright and landed on her bottom.

'Oh my god it's true, it's all true; this is the place. This is where the rocks fell. This is where they all became trapped.' She pulled herself back to her feet and shuffled backward quickly.

She tapped Mr. Fuzzy lightly. 'Do you go any brighter?' she said and continued to tap him on the head. He shone a little brighter and she pointed him in the direction of the wall. It was boulder after boulder on top of each other, at least a hundred feet tall.

She saw something. It was a little way up, but she knew she could climb up, and she knew she could reach it; so she did. She placed Mr. Fuzzy on her shoulder and made her way up to the funny looking object that was protruding the blockade. As she got closer, it became clearer. It was a greyish white colour. It was long and sharp looking. It was extremely large.

'Just a bit further.' She said as she climbed. Until, she was just below it. She reached out and placed her hand on the edge of the object. Its surface was smooth and had odd shaped holes in the top. She pulled herself up with it, but it was not lodged in firmly enough. It slipped out of the rock and fell to the floor. Soria nearly fell. She clambered to maintain her grip, but slipped and slid down, until she hit the floor with a thud. She landed awkwardly, but remained unharmed.

'Ouch!' She let out a sarcastic laugh and turned to Mr. Fuzzy, who was also unharmed. He had landed softly like a fallen balloon. 'Are you okay?' she asked.

He looked at her and smiled. 'Good, I'm glad you're okay. Now let's look at what this thing is.' She walked over to it for a closer look and gestured for Mr. Fuzzy to walk over to her. As he got closer, the large grey object became clearer. It was no object at all, it was a skull, a very large and very sinister looking skull.

Soria took a step back and gasped. It was unmistakably a lycunflame skull. Even dead it looked terrifying. Large jagged teeth in a gaping jaw. It's expression was frozen in time. One bite from such a creature could have torn her in two.

'You know what, Mr. Fuzzy, I don't think I like the stories of the lycunflame anymore. If this is what they looked like. I'm glad I'll never bump into one. So long as they are on the other side of this wall, and I am on this side, I'll remain a very happy person. I would not like to lead the people against something like that.' She was short on breath and beginning to panic. 'I think we had better leave now. Even if they aren't alive anymore, I don't want to find out. There is clearly no way to get up the mountain and that is probably for the best; come on.'

Soria left the cave swiftly and the skull was left on the floor. She had no interest in ever showing anyone such a thing. It was frightfully easy to forget it ever existed and walk away.

They had exited the cave. Soria looked over Athia, disappointed. She was disappointed that she was unable to make it to the red dragon. She was disappointed in herself for being too weak to make the climb. The youngling in her would have spat at her feet. She would have looked at her disgusted. But, who was the disappointment? The five-year-old Soria who stood atop the first mountain peak of Athia, or the seventeen-year-old Soria, who stood atop the first mountain peak.

The former would have stormed the cave, regardless of what laid beyond the boulders. She would have shrugged at the skull of the creatures of the past, long since dead and clawed her way through the rubble to reach the other side. This Soria was contemplating returning, a failure, and offering the title of chieftainess to Aylen.

'No!' she shouted into the wind. 'This will not do. I will not be defeated. I am Soria, Chieftainess of Athia, and I will not allow my tribe to suffer. I have made it this far, and I will continue to the top, one way or another, until I reach the guardian dragon. Then, I will return with the resolution to this crisis we now face.'

She turned back and faced the cavern entrance for the third time. 'I'm going back. Are you with me?' she said to her companion.

She stepped dead centre of the entrance, and stood in front of the dragon statues. Just as she was about to step forward, the ground shook uncontrollably. An earthquake rattled the floor beneath her feet and took them from under her. She rose to her feet quickly and steadied herself. The ground continued to rumble and rocks rolled down the mountain side. She picked up Mr. Fuzzy, who was about to be crushed by one of the rolling boulders, dove out of the way and landed awkwardly. Her arm bruised instantly and she let out a painful cry. She squeezed him tight and curled into a ball with her eyes scrunched.

'What is happening!' she yelled.

Never had Athia had an earthquake in modern times. It was unheard of. The mountains were not actively volcanic and the land had been unaltered for centuries.

The shaking continued for several minutes and the ground beneath her cracked like thunder and had begun to split. She kept her eyes closed and waited in a foetal position for the ordeal to be over.

Chapter Ten

T
he shaking stopped, and she dared not move at first. The ground may have stopped shaking, but her body continued to do so. Slowly, Soria opened her arms and released her companion from her clutches. Her intent was to keep him protected, yet she had almost crushed him in her embrace. He fell out of her arms, luckily unharmed, albeit a bit dizzy. He swayed as he walked and Soria grabbed him before he fell into the crack that had formed in the floor.

She looked at it curiously. 'Look at that.' She said. She followed the crack with her eyes, down the mountain and beyond what her sight would permit her to see. 'It must lead all the way back to the village. What could have caused this?' she rubbed her arm, which was as purple as a ripe plum. 'Ouch. That hurts. But, I guess it could be worse.' She looked at the huge boulders that landed a few feet from where she fell. 'Much worse.' She added.

Mr. Fuzzy was shaking too. His fur stood on end and he was vibrating like the ground was still moving. Soria picked up her companion and stroked his fur flat. She had never been any good at comforting anyone before, yet she made a conscious effort to soothe him. 'There, there. It's okay. We are okay.' She said gracelessly, like she was only impersonating kindness. His fur flattened and he stopped trembling.

Soria looked at the entrance to the cavern. 'Well.' She said. 'It looks like that settles it. We have no choice now. We must proceed. Or we will have no home to go back to.' She popped Mr. Fuzzy on her shoulder and started towards the entrance.

Then, she stopped. She heard a deep grumbling noise. 'Was that you?' she asked. 'Or, was that me? Are you hungry? Am I hungry'

The grumbling noise came from ahead. It was not their stomachs calling for food.

She stared intently into the infinite blackness of the cave entrance. It looked as though something was moving, or was it her eyes playing tricks on her, she couldn't quite tell. 'Hello.' She called.

She heard a growling and a snarling. So, she took a step back. 'Is anyone there?' she called again, but received no reply.

The growling and snarling grew louder and sharper. Hungry eyes stared back at her through the darkness. Large slanted blood red eyes, that were accompanied by sharp burning red teeth. 'Do you see what I am seeing?' she asked worried. 'Or, was I hit on the head?'

Her companion, for the first time, did not smile. *Is that you shaking?* She thought. *Or, is it me, or both of us. Please tell me that it's all in my head.*

The eyes grew larger, or whatever they were attached to was getting closer. She moved back at the same pace that the eyes teetered forward. A wet snout peered out from the cavern entrance and entered the light. A large snout which housed large burning fangs. *It can't be.* She thought.

A deep growl came from deep within the cave; there was more than one of them. She did not need it to come any closer, as she knew exactly what it was. It continued to stare at her with its hungry eyes. It seemed to be savouring the moment. It tasted the air and appeared to smile. A large pointed tongue flopped out of the side of its mouth and dripped drool on the floor. The air was hot, so it evaporated on the spot. The air was hotter now than it had ever been, as the midday sun burned high in the sky.

She dared not move. It was a staring contest. The creature in the cavern did not take a further step, so Soria took a step further back. She heard a large growl and the creature leaped from the spot at her. She raised her arms to protect herself and awaited her fate. *This is it. My time is up.* She thought.

She felt a biting at her skin and was instantly cold, as though she had already passed away from the shock. *This is what death must feel like*, she thought. It was not like what she expected. She began to shiver, and goose pimples rose to the surface of her forearms and legs. She lowered her arms and a gust of air bit at her cheeks. Her eyes had begun to open. A bright white filled her sight, and she left them half shut in fear of being blinded. But it was not light that she could see. It was a strange powdered white texture. She lowered her arms completely and took in the scenery. Specs of deep, dark green pierced the white. She was in a forest, but it was not like any forest she had ever seen before. The trees stood taller than any tree in Athia, and were greener than she ever thought possible. Glass crystals dangled like chandeliers from the branches and were dripping in the heat of the sun. Although, it was not hot, it was quite the opposite. Soria wrapped her arms around her chest and attempted to warm herself with little effect.

Every passing gust nipped at her face, arms and legs. She ran to shelter behind the nearest of the ferns, but it offered little protection against the chill. *Where am I?* She thought.

Then her attention was drawn away from herself. She could not see her companion anywhere. She began to troll through the thick, wet, white powder. It squelched under her feet and seeped through the thin material that embalmed her feet. She did not have the correct footwear for such a place, nor did she have clothes warm enough to combat the freezing temperatures. However, she was not concerned about herself, she just knew that she had to find her companion. If she was, indeed, still alive, she did not want to brave this strange land without him.

A scream. A loud scream drifted through the trees. It was a girl's scream. Soria stopped and listened. She heard nothing. All was silent. Then, again she heard it. A loud scream not so far away. It was most definitely a girl screaming.

Not knowing where she was, where her companion was, or what had just happened, she ran towards it. She did not concern herself with what was causing the girl to yell in such a way, and only wished to find her, so that she could find out where she was.

She ran as fast as her legs could carry her up a steep hill. A large branch sticking out slapped her arm. The purpling bruise began to pulsate. *Definitely still alive then,* she thought, and unsure of whether or not that was a good thing.

155

She could hear something else as she got closer. She could hear something very familiar, very familiar indeed. It was that of a creature snarling. The sound of a creature that she thought she had just escaped. Except, instead of stopping and running away, she ran faster, harder, and headfirst into the danger, as though she was compelled to do so.

An opening appeared in the trees, so she ran toward it and burst out to see who was under attack.

There was a girl, around the same age, standing backed up against a tree. She had bright sparkly white hair. She wore a dress of sorts, not like Soria's, as it was much thicker, and some thick boots. She was clearly more equipped for the weather than Soria was. She held a dagger of sorts; only, she had never seen such a vicious weapon as she had never really seen a weapon at all. The Athianne had tools they used to build tents and extract vegetation, yes indeed; some even sharp enough to be considered useful as a weapon, but they had no weapons as such.

The girl pointed the blade out in front of her, and stabbed at the air with little conviction. She faced it toward a wolf. It was not like any wolf she had ever seen before. The face that was coming out of the cavern was the closest she came to witnessing anything so ferocious, and even that was a blur. It was oddly coloured; almost the same colour as the girls hair. Its fangs were like broken shards of glass from a smashed bottle, that had been picked up from the ground and forced back into its mouth awkwardly.

Soria picked up a large fallen branch off the floor. It was a thick branch with smaller ones sticking out of it. It looked too heavy for anyone of Soria's size to wield, but her adrenaline kicked in. She picked up the log for a branch and hurled herself at the beast, waving it wildly and screaming. It diverted the wolfs attention, just enough for the girl to plunge the dagger into the side of its neck. It let out a howl and tried to turn and run. Soria cracked the beast on its snout, then continued to hit it until it fell to the ground.

The two girls looked down at the wolf, who was most assuredly dead, and panted with exhaustion. 'What is it?' Said Soria, as she gasped for breath.

The other girl, looked at Soria for a moment. 'Just a common wolf.' She said. 'We have them all over Glacia.'

'Excuse me?' said Soria. 'You have them all over where now?' Soria looked lost for words and the other girl looked unsure how to answer, what she thought was a question that was not in need of one.

She grabbed the girl by her shoulders, then forced her against the thick trunk of the tree behind her. 'Where did you say we were? Tell me now. I am Soria, Chieftainess of Athia, and I demand you tell me what this strange place is. Am I dead? Speak now!'

The girl brushed off Soria's hands and pushed her back. 'Unhand me at once, Soria, Chieftainess of Athia. Firstly, thank you for the assist. Secondly, though, you are not in Athia now. You are in Glacia. And I, Ohmiya, am Chieftainess of these lands you walk in.'

Soria looked stunned, as she had no idea what Glacia was, or where it was, nor how she came to be there. 'Glacia?' she replied.

Ohmiya looked slightly irritated that she had to repeat herself again. But she could see that poor Soria was in a state of hysteria, so she obliged. 'Yes, Glacia. Land of the Glacianne tribe, which is under the protection of our guardian, the white dragon.'

Soria smiled. 'Wait. You are telling me, that I am on the opposite side of the Sapphire Stream. The land of the white dragon. Ha. You are joking aren't you? Of course you are. I really am dead.' Soria begun rambling like a crazy person.

Ohmiya grabbed her shoulder. 'Ouch!' Shouted Soria.

'Sorry.' Replied Ohmiya. 'But, wait a minute. You said, "the opposite side of the Sapphire Stream." Does that mean you're from the other side?' Ohmiya interrupted herself and asked another question instead. 'No wait, answer me this instead. Are you from the side, where the red dragon is supposed to live? That place is called Athia?' Ohmiya continued speaking and didn't wait for an answer. 'That is so cool, I always wanted to know what it's like on the other side, what the people are like, what they wear, everything. You have to tell me everything.'

Both girls looked at each other. Soria, looked confused and aggravated. Ohmiya looked excitedly curious. But neither one had time to exchange any further dialogue at that moment.

'Wait. Hold that thought. I need to find Snowflake. He seemed to vanish in a flash of white light and I don't know where he went. I need to find him first. Then we can talk.' Ohmiya grabbed the girls hand tightly and began to walk briskly.

Soria snatched her hand from Ohmiya's. 'Wait, I need to find someone too. I don't have time to help you find this, Snowflake, person.'

Ohmiya stopped. 'He's not a person, he's my companion. We get them when we are younger from our guardian. But, he is important to me. I would never forgive myself if anything happened to him. Who are you looking for? Maybe we can help each other?'

Soria was shivering in the cold and turning bluer than the bruise on her arm. 'I don't need any help from anyone.' She said through chattering teeth.

Ohmiya smiled sarcastically. 'No, of course not.' She said. 'Because you look fit to take on anything in that state. Even the yeti's would tremble before you in fear.'

Soria looked puzzled. 'What is a yeti?' she asked

Ohmiya laughed. 'Really? You don't have those? My guess is you would probably make it three minutes before you are torn apart, disembowelled, or, if you are extremely lucky, eaten whole.'

Soria tried to keep a straight face and act as though she was tough as nails. She did not know this person, and she had never shown any sign of weakness in front of anyone. This, she thought to herself, was not going to be the first. However, her caramel brown skin began to turn pale at the thought of anything eating her whole, as a best-case scenario.

Soria opened her mouth, and was about to retort something, that would make her seem like the invincible warrior princess she perceived herself to be. But her words were intercepted by Ohmiya. 'I'm kidding, of course. A strong young woman like yourself might make it; hmm maybe five minutes. Nevertheless, we will be far safer if we travel together. Besides, you need a navigator and I wouldn't mind some company on my journey.' She said smugly.

Ohmiya was seldom refused by anyone, as she had never met anyone that disliked her company. The Glacianne people revered her, as she was so abnormally pleasant, it was hard to say a bad word about her. She was often sought out by her people for her company, and would sometimes evade her tribe for some much-needed solitude. So, Soria was a breath of fresh air, a challenge, and Ohmiya liked to accomplish anything that wasn't easy. Although she planned on making the journey alone, she had a feeling that something had brought the pair together. And, she was not about to allow her to leave so easily.

She proceeded to talk without allowing Soria to speak, hoping she would submit to her influence, and possibly agree to follow her in fear of her being followed anyway. 'And, if you have any chance of finding who you are looking for, you will need me too, I'm guessing.' She said.

Soria huffed and puffed with discontent. 'Fine.' She submitted. Although she acted as irritated as she would before anyone's company but Solis', she too felt as though leaving Ohmiya, would be poor judgement on her part. *Maybe this isn't such a bad idea. Maybe some company is what I need too. Plus, she is right,* she pondered, *I have no idea where I am, or how to return home, so walking the place alone would be foolhardy.*

Ohmiya grinned a big grin. 'Great. Friends?' she said, and held out her hand.

Soria scoffed at her offer of a handshake. 'No. We are partners until we no longer have use for one another.' But, what she really felt was a warming sensation through her whole body. Her heart raced and cheeks went a rose red, which shone brightly against her frost-bitten skin. She had never had a friend before, and would not likely have expected an offer of friendship from anyone. Yet, Ohmiya, a complete stranger, held her hand out and offered it willingly.

Ohmiya, was hard to offend. She was also unable to withhold her tongue from speaking her mind. 'Fair enough. A bit rude, but I'll take it. We are partners until we go our separate ways. But on the way, you might as well tell me all about Athia.' Ohmiya pleaded through pleasing eyes.

'Fine. But, only until I find my companion. Then we're gone.' Said Soria.

Ohmiya's eyes widened. 'You have a companion too? What's it like? Do you get one from your guardian?' she asked.

'It, is actually a, he.' She replied. 'Or, at least I think he is a, he. I never really gave it much thought before. It's hard to tell. And, yes, we get them when we are five. It's kind of like a rite of passage. He's small and furry, and up until now, when I found out he could do more than simply smile, a giant pain in my behind. What's yours like?'

Ohmiya wondered how anyone could be so cruel about their companion. 'I'm sure he's wonderful. They are all special.' She said. And, Soria rolled her eyes. 'Snowflake is small, and cute and cuddly. He kind of looks like a giant snowflake, except he's small in comparison to most companions. He doesn't really have legs though, or arms, just little feet that poke out of the bottom. So, he's not very fast, and just waddles around. He doesn't really do much, but he has an adorable smile. He's...' Soria ended her sentence and they both said the same word at the same time, 'unique.'

Soria looked at Ohmiya curiously. Her mind had begun to rewind and concentrate on certain facts. 'Where did you say you were heading again?' she quizzed Ohmiya.

Ohmiya looked thrilled that Soria was engaging in conversation. 'I didn't. But, if you're really interested, I'm on the way to see the white dragon. There has been lots of strange goings on around here and I…' Ohmiya continued to speak, but Soria had left the conversation and entered into her own thoughts.

So, we are both on our way to speak to our guardians for similar reasons. We both have companions that sound equally useless. I end up here, miraculously, just as I am about to be mauled to death by a wild animal, and bump into a girl, who is about to be mauled to death by a wild animal. I don't believe in coincidences. This means something. Even if she can't see it, I know that this means something.

'I have changed my mind.' Soria blurted out as Ohmiya was mid-sentence.

Ohmiya looked startled and a little upset. 'You don't want to come with me?'

Soria smiled. 'Don't look so down. I have changed my mind about leaving. I am not just going to come along with you until I find Mr. Fuzzy. I am going to help you on your quest, to do whatever it is you are doing.'

Ohmiya looked stunned. 'What? Really? You… Want to join me?'

'Yes, I want to join you.' Soria replied, smiling through gritted teeth. 'It's like you said, I probably wouldn't last five minutes here alone; I don't know where on earth I am and clearly have no way of getting home. My only option is to follow you. The dragon guardians are connected, if the story is true, so maybe yours will be able to help me return home.' Said Soria.

'Well, great. That's great!' Ohmiya said, still a little shocked. But what shocked her most, was the name Soria spoke of. *Mr. Fuzzy?* She thought. *I'm sure that name sounds familiar. I don't know why, but it does. Weird.*

'So?' said Soria.

Ohmiya, still lost for words, had stopped walking and talking, which was highly unusual for her. 'So?' she replied.

'So, which way do we go? Where do you think our companions could have gotten to?' asked Soria, abruptly.

'I don't really know.' Said Ohmiya. 'When the flash of light appeared, I was a fair bit further up the mountain. It seems to have sent me backward, down the mountain. We already passed these parts. So I think that it was more likely, I, who was transported down here, and not Snowflake. Maybe he is where I was, and I was brought here. So, we should probably head back to where I was. It's about an hour's hike in that direction.'

Soria started walking. 'Great. Let's get going then.' She said.

Ohmiya grabbed her hand again and pulled her back. The bruise on her arm hurt even more now than it had before. 'Ouch! Will you stop doing that. I am clearly hurt.'

'Sorry.' Said Ohmiya, earnestly. 'It's just, we can't go back the way we went the first time around. I kind of left an angry yeti that way. Who headed back this way. He could be anywhere around here now. We're best off going this way. I wasn't kidding about the, being torn apart. They are pretty vicious and you wouldn't want to run into one. This way would be safer. It may take a little while longer, but we have more chance of making it up the mountain alive at least.'

Soria looked irritated at spending any more time than she had to on the journey ahead. But definitely liked the idea of staying alive, a lot more than being torn limb from limb by an angry monster.

She shivered again and fog was forming with her every breath. 'You couldn't go any further in your current attire anyway. Look at you. You're as white the ground beneath your feet.' Said Ohmiya, and she quickly took off her backpack. Inside she had a spare set of Glacianne clothes, the ones she would ordinarily have worn at that time of year. She handed them over to Soria. 'Here, wear these. Any longer in that flimsy cloth you call clothing and you'll reduce to nothing more than a frozen statue.' Ohmiya chuckled to herself.

Soria snatched the outfit from Ohmiya. She inspected the material with her forefinger and thumb. The thick mammoth skin was also soft to the touch. She smiled as she rubbed it against her skin, then turned to Ohmiya. 'Thanks, I guess.'

Ohmiya placed her hands on her hips. 'You're welcome, I guess.'
She replied.

Soria raised an eye bow, unimpressed. 'Well?'

'Well, what?' replied Ohmiya.

Soria used her finger to infer that Ohmiya should turn around.
'Avert your eyes while I change. I cannot have a complete stranger
watch me undress.'

'Oh, I'm sorry. I just assumed you would put them on over the
top of what you are already wearing.' Ohmiya said. *Considering,
that what you are wearing could barely be considered clothing
anyway.* She thought.

Ohmiya turned away and Soria quickly changed, scrunching her
old clothes into a ball and stuffing them into her tiny bag.

Soria pointed ahead. 'Okay then, lead the way.' She said.

Ohmiya looked her up and down. 'Something is missing.' She
said, and scratched her head. She looked down at the soggy cloth
that was wrapped around her feet. 'Yes, I almost forgot.' She said.
'You can't wear those on your feet, or by the time we get to where
we are going, they will surely have dropped off.' And, she pulled out
a pair of boots from her bag. 'Try these on, you look about my size.'
Although clothes were made to fit the person that made them, it was
lucky for Soria, that her and Ohmiya were practically the same
proportions.

Although Soria felt awkward in the heavy new outfit she donned, the warmth was very much welcomed.

'I don't believe it. The air is colder than I ever thought possible, yet inside these odd garments, it feels as warm as the Athianne plains. What are they made from?' Soria asked.

'Mammoth hide.' Ohmiya replied.

Soria's skin had once again begun to drain of colour. 'I'm wearing dead animal?' she asked. 'No, I'm wearing the arse of a dead animal?'

'Of course, it's the toughest part of the mammoth. And it makes for excellent protection against the freezing temperatures. It gets colder the higher we climb.

'What is wrong with you people? Why would you kill an animal? And for clothing no less.' Soria said, horrified.

'How else are we supposed to make clothes, or eat for that matter?' Ohmiya looked puzzled.

Soria looked as though she was about to vomit. 'You eat… you eat the animals, and then wear them?'

Ohmiya chuckled sympathetically. 'Of course we do. Nothing edible grows here. All we have is the animals to live off. All the animals here eat each other. It's just the way it goes around here. I don't like it any more than you do, but it's what we have to do to survive. Otherwise we would starve and die. What do you do for food, and how do you make the clothes you wear?'

Soria looked less accusingly at Ohmiya. 'We eat from the land and we make clothes from the fur of the creatures. I don't recall an Athianne ever having to kill another person, or animal alike, in modern times. It's just unheard of. But, I guess things work differently around here.' She looked at the vast white land with no sign of vegetation; just tall green trees and a bright white floor.

'Believe me, if we didn't have to eat meat, I wouldn't. I even refused to go hunting, as I could not bear to see another animal suffer.' Tears filled her eyes as she thought about the ox. She still believed her actions were merciful. But the pain she felt taking its life would haunt her forever.

Soria could see she had upset her, yet she was not good at displaying empathy. She placed her hand on her shoulder. 'I'm sorry.' She said. 'It is not my place to judge another's way of life. Let's just set off shall we? You can ask me all that you wish to know about where I come from.'

Ohmiya picked up her head and smiled at this. She set off with a skip in her step as she walked ahead. 'This is going to be so much fun.' She said, excited. 'So, tell me all about Athia. I want to know everything.' She said.

'Yes I'm sure it will, and I have no doubt you do.' Soria sighed. 'What do you want to know?'

Then, both girls set off up the mountain together in search of their companions.

Chapter Eleven

A thia's lands were scorching. Etherflame were ablaze in the heat of the afternoon sun. The adults were hidden away from the heat in their huts and tents. The young were struggling, too. The heat felt hotter than fire and the land had begun to crack, creating deep crevices through the village; some so big, that they swallowed homes whole. The earth shook spontaneously and caused the cracks to deepen.

The tents that housed the food, clothes and other valuable supplies had been sucked up by the ground. Argon's companion swooped into the crevices to retrieve lost items.

Aylen and Torch rounded up the gatherers that had ventured out the night before. Athianne would often spend days at a time in search for food, which sometimes led them farther away from the camp than they might have liked. However, with no natural enemies, there was no need to fear sleeping under the stars for a night or two. Yet, today was not a natural occurrence.

The heat attacked from above and the ground attacked from below. And what was coming for them was far worse than both. The lycunflame had escaped their prison and were waiting for the sun to sleep. When the moon was full, was when they were going to make their way down the mountain in search of food. The village may have been half a day's hike for a human. But blood thirsty wolves could travel much, much faster. Their senses were fine tuned to taste the scent of Athianne from miles away. The villagers scents travelled up the mountain like a tasty teaser before dinner, which had the lycunflame licking their lips.

The Athianne, just like the Glacianne, were in a state of disarray. Their home was in ruin and their lives in jeopardy. Both peoples, had their fates resting in the hands of two young women.

Unlike the Glacianne, though, Soria had not left with the knowing of her elders. She had crept away from her home, without so much as a goodbye.

Argon, and her parents were searching frantically for her in the midst of the chaos. She had not left home sound of mind and they feared the worst for their future leader. They were the only adults up and about. Her father and mother had to abandon their search after a short while, as they were not feeling at all well.

'Can we trust that you will not rest until she is found?' they demanded without a care for the safety of those who they were commanding. Soria had gained her nonappreciative tone from her parents. Although times of great crisis had never arose until now, and their demands were usually more trivial, they cared little for the life of Argon, or any other villager for that matter. The people were merely tools, who were there to serve their leaders and their family.

Argon, however, was not concerned with receiving praise. He, too, cared for Soria as much as Solis had. So, the request was unnecessary as he would have gladly searched for her until his last breath was taken.

Aylen had returned with the lost gatherers. Her and Torch were a formidable pair. She had grown into a strong young woman. Even if the heat had bothered her, she would not likely have shown it. She had gained such traits from observing Soria in her youth, as she wished for the same level of fear and respect. However, as Soria's companion looked less formidable, her confidence and conviction dwindled over time. Aylen then took the mantel from her. Aylen already had something that Soria did not; followers. This alone would not have been enough to threaten Soria's position. Yet, with Torch by her side, she had the strength to command their reverence.

Argon called her over. She galloped over on Torch's back as though riding a stallion. 'We haven't seen the young chieftainess since last night.' He said. 'You and I must look for her, now that the villagers are all safe. The earthquakes seem to have stopped for the time being, so now is the time to go and look for her.'

Aylen rolled her eyes. 'Do we really? I am sure that our future leader is more than capable of taking care of herself.' She said in a disrespectful manor.

Argon was not amused. 'This is no time for any childish display of dominance. You may have grown into yourself little one. But you will not talk about the future chieftainess of this tribe in such a manor, not in my presence. Do you understand?' he pointed his finger jaggedly at her.

Aylen had grown cocky, but she would not likely take on Argon, even if she would have joked about being the strongest of the Athianne. He would likely have killed her and Torch, or died trying, if someone should suggest a legitimate threat against Soria and her family. 'Where do we start?' she replied sheepishly.

He looked up toward the mountain peaks. 'Her father seems to think she may have headed towards the mountain tops. He thinks she may try something extreme. I'm not sure where else she may have gone to. But, as most paths lead towards the mountain anyway, I suggest that we head that way. Hopefully we will find her safe and bring her home. Then, we can work out how to resolve this mess.'

Aylen never spoke a word. She nodded in affirmation and set off ahead. Torch was as fast as a forest fire. Argon ordered his companion to follow Aylen, Then he set of slowly behind them.

His phoenix soared high above the ground, until it was no more than a blemish, a mere blotch, in the blue of the sky.

***

The Glacianne tribe were safely behind the spires that formed the wall around their city. Not one had fallen, not yet. The earth did not quake west of the Sapphire Stream. It only had done once weeks before. The only, earth-shattering, noises came from the falling city within the Glacianne walls. The scales that had stood for hundreds of years, and been home to many, were falling faster than the snow was melting away. All the Glacianne could do is watch on as their homes were destroyed under the weight of the huge scales of the white dragon's skin.

The creatures were not deterred from taking a closer look at the carnage. Lurking in the open plains, creatures were collecting in large numbers. They could smell the fear of the Glacianne. Yeti's brawled on the east side; fighting over who would be the first to taste human flesh. Wolves fought playfully and awaited nightfall, as, like their flame fanged cousins on the other side of the Sapphire Stream, they liked to hunt at night; hunger was all that brought them out through the day, if they hadn't managed to successfully kill at night.

The Glacianne hunters in the watch towers grew nervous, as they could only watch the numbers of the creatures increase. Another stunt like earlier would have likely ended in fatality for one or more of their people, so they remained firmly behind their walls. The spires were holding, so long as the ground did not quake. So, for that moment, they had nothing to fear. Even the yeti would not try plough through the sharpened pikes that were spread evenly around the wall. They may have seemed like mindless monsters, but they were not completely without intelligence. An easy meal was preferable, over one that would end in injury. An injured yeti was a vulnerable yeti, as, if another was hungry enough, they would happily resort to cannibalism.

Freya had not slept, and she would not have slept without first knowing that Ohmiya was safe. Her mind was torn. *I hope she is okay, please be okay,* was the ever-continuous thought that plagued her mind. Also, she thought about what was happening outside the walls, and was plotting their defence, weighing up all possible outcomes; the good and the unthinkable. Daylight was burning rapidly, and she knew that the creatures outside the walls would be seeking weak points and holes in their defences. It was as though they could sense that the people were no longer protected. The Glacianne had always been on top of the food chain, and nature was in tune with the balance. Yet, with the white dragon's outer shell falling fast, they could sense that something was wrong, and they could sense that the Glacianne were vulnerable.

***

The mountainous terrain seemed tougher to climb than before. The route Ohmiya had taken before was shorter, and she was less tired. Now, however, she had already gone through several close shaves and was forced to take the longest route. Even if they were to make it to the cave of the white dragon, their journey was far from over, as no one had ever entered.

Soria had regained her colour and was feeling more like herself, albeit a little agitated.

Ohmiya had asked her an intolerable amount of questions. Her patience had worn thin and she had begun to give shortened answers to the questions. One, or two words, but very few more than was necessary.

Ohmiya stopped talking and thought for a moment. *Thank the guardian, she must have run out of things to ask me,* thought Soria, and she sighed with relief. 'So…' Ohmiya began with another question and Soria exhaled eccentrically with despair. 'So, where were you going when you were brought here anyway? What were you doing?' she asked.

'I…' Soria stopped talking. 'It's none of your business.' She snapped.

Ohmiya looked cross. 'Why are you like this all the time? Are all Athianne like you?'

'Like me?' she probed.

Ohmiya, as she never had done, did not mince her words. 'Rude, obnoxious and ignorant.' She said.

Soria gasped in offence. It may have been almost entirely true, but not many dared speak so candidly in front of her. Or, they hadn't until recently. 'How dare you talk to me like that?' she said.

'I'll talk to you however I see fit. I saved you from the wolf, I give you warm clothes and I'm helping you, although I don't know why, from a fate worse than death. You want to go alone and face all the wonders that Glacia offers at night, then be my guest. But, I assure you, if you think that wolf from earlier was bad, you will not like what else comes out at night.' Ohmiya began to cry. She had been holding back her feelings from what had happened to her father, in fear she may fall apart completely and not complete her quest. But Soria had pushed her too far.

Soria realised that she had been less than grateful for the assistance Ohmiya had offered. She also realised that this was someone that had offered her friendship; the only person in an entire lifetime that had tolerated her for longer than was reasonably necessary. And, Ohmiya was not even part of her tribe. So, she had no real reason for offering kindness of any sort. But, even so, she did anyway, willingly.

Ohmiya continued to sob. Soria knew she had been less than kind. But she also knew that she could not possibly be this upset about her unwillingness to participate in answering her endless stream of questions. She placed her hand on the small of her back. 'I'm sorry.' She said.

'It's alright. It's not you.' Ohmiya replied.

Soria knew there was more to her tears. She did not really want to ask, but was attempting to be a better person, and forced herself to seem concerned. 'What is it?' she asked.

Ohmiya hissed at her. 'You don't really want to know.' She said, as she could sense Soria could not care less.

Soria could see how much she was hurting, and, if only for a second, she felt guilty. She felt guilty that she had the ability to make someone else feel better, even if she was reluctant to. So, she persisted. 'Really, I am sorry. Please, tell me what happened? I am interested.' She said.

Ohmiya stopped crying for a moment. 'It's the reason I'm on my way up this treacherous mountain. It's the reason I'm trying to get to our guardian. My father.' She stopped herself from crying further and wiped the tears from her eyes. 'My father passed away recently. Like, really recently. There was nothing I could do to save him. But, our home is also at risk of falling to pieces. It crumbles as we speak. And the only way to stop it is to get to the cave of our guardian, and to find out what is happening from the white dragon himself. He is the only one who can help us now. Otherwise, I may as well not go home. Or, I will just be returning a failure, to a ruined city. I cannot go back a failure.'

Soria could not believe it. That the exact same thing was happening Glacia. She could see something strange was going on, and that their fates were more closely linked than she would like to have admitted. But, now, hearing what Ohmiya was saying, it was hard to dismiss the fact. They were destined to meet in such a way.

Soria knelt down by Ohmiya, who was still weeping on her knees in the slush. 'I understand.' She said. 'I know how you're feeling right now.'

'How could you?' Ohmiya replied.

'Because, believe it or not, my story is not too dissimilar from your own. I was also on a journey to seek out our guardian, the red dragon. Our land, it's heating up. It's so hot, that even the Athianne cannot stand it, and we can place our hand over a naked flame a short time without so much as a burn. My people are dying. One in particular...' Soria held back her tears, then continued. 'One person in particular, someone I was very close to, the only person I was close to, passed away. She was old, but I don't believe it was her time to go. She was taken from me too early. I was supposed to take over as chieftainess of our tribe yesterday, and on my first day as leader, I left. I left to seek out guidance from the red dragon, because I had no idea what else to do. And, I couldn't even do that. I am a failure.' She said.

Ohmiya stopped crying. She was amazed that Soria had finally opened up. She could feel, as well as hear the words she spoke. She could feel her pain. She could empathise with her. They were the same in so many ways, yet so completely different in others. 'I doubt that you are a failure.' She said.

'Well you'd be the first.' Soria replied.

'You have not failed yet.' Ohmiya stood with conviction. 'I don't believe we found each other by accident. I think our meeting happened for a reason. I don't believe you have failed at your mission. I just think that you were maybe going in the wrong direction, so fate brought you here.' She said.

She held out her hand for Soria. And, for the first time, for the first time in her life, Soria offered her hand in return. Ohmiya lifted

180

her firmly from the ground. 'Our lands are connected. I don't know exactly how, and I don't think anyone truly does. But, I believe that if the story about the two dragons is true, then they are both connected, even now. If the white dragon can help Glacia, I am sure he can help Athia, too, and your people. We may have both failed alone, but together we will not. We will both return home successful, with the resolution to this, that is happening to both our homes.'

Soria smiled. It was still only half a smile, but it was a genuine smile. 'You are right, I know you are right. We will do this, together.' She agreed. 'And, I saved you.'

Ohmiya raised an eyebrow. 'What?' she asked.

Soria smiled again. 'You said, that it was you that saved me from the wolf. When, I think, it was actually, I, who saved you.' She said.

Ohmiya laughed. 'Okay, you remember it differently, but that's fine. We can agree to disagree.'

Soria laughed also. 'Fair enough.' She said.

The air grew colder as the daylight was fading. The evening temperature dipped, but the sun was not ready to surrender to the moon just yet. They needed to make it to the cave entrance before nightfall, and both needed to find their companions. Mr. Fuzzy and Snowflake were still nowhere to be seen and both girls were frightfully aware of this. So, together, they continued up to the mountain.

Chapter Twelve

T he wolves howled at the setting sun. A frosty breeze blew fiercely up the Glacianne mountains and the slushy floor froze instantly. 'Watch your step.' Said Ohmiya, as Soria scrambled for the nearest branch to maintain her balance. 'The floor gets slippery at night.'

Ohmiya grabbed two small ferns from the floor, that had fallen from the tree, then pulled some string from her bag. 'Here.' She said. Ohmiya tied the ferns to the bottom of Soria's shoes to make them grip to the floor.

Soria, looking less ungrateful, thanked her. 'Thank you. That's quite impressive.' She said.

Ohmiya smiled sardonically. 'Was that a compliment?' she asked.

Soria did not like, and had never liked, being mocked. 'I was merely stating that your resourcefulness is impressive.' And she smiled happily now that she was able to walk without falling.

Ohmiya laughed. 'I'll take it, and you are welcome. We are trained from birth to make use of the land and all its resources. It's a shame that we don't seem to be able to make anything that can brighten up the night. The stars are the only light we have.'

Soria looked puzzled. 'Why don't you just make a fire at night? That should brighten up the darkest of places.'

'Fire? Here? That's not possible, it's far too cold. Nothing here could burn for longer than a few seconds at best.' Ohmiya replied, and laughed at the notion.

Soria stopped, Ohmiya beckoned her to keep walking. 'What are you stopping for? We aren't that far away now; we can't stop yet.' She said.

Soria had a glint of smugness in her expression. 'Just wait a second.' She said. 'It's getting too dark to see and soon we will not be able to see our hands in front of our faces. If there are truly horrors that lurk in the night here. I would sure like to see them coming, and avoid them completely if at all possible. I have something from my homeland, that once alight, will not burn out or dim; not even under these extremes.' And, she drew out one of the Etherflame's.

Ohmiya was intrigued, but sceptical. 'That's great. But, how on earth do you intend to make fire from a flower, and how do you intend to light it?' she asked.

Soria looked pleased that there was something she could show Ohmiya, as she had begun to feel inferior. 'I guess that there are some things that they don't teach you here then. And, I was beginning to think you knew everything.'

'Okay smarty pants. Show me.' Ohmiya replied, delighted that they seemed to be bonding.

Soria withdrew two sticks from her backpack. She had begun to rub them hard together. A light grey smoke appeared from the broken branches. But, then, she had to stop. Her arm was pulsating and she cried out in pain. 'Ouch!' She shouted. 'That really hurts.'

'Give them here then.' Said Ohmiya. 'I'll do it. How hard can it be?'

Soria looked unimpressed. 'I doubt you will be able to.' She snarled. 'It's not as easy as it looks.' But, as Soria was talking, Ohmiya had already picked up the sticks and begun to rub them together. Within a few seconds, flames flickered and the branches were alight. Ohmiya had rarely seen fire, and was dazzled by its beauty. She stared at it, was entranced by it.

'Ohmiya!' Soria shouted loudly at her. 'Be careful with that, it is really hot, it could burn you.' Ohmiya dropped the sticks, as the flames had crawled up and nearly burned the tips of her fingers. Luckily, the sticks landed on the Etherflame, and it began to burn as bright as the sun. 'You see, easy.' She said.

Ohmiya reached out to grab it, but Soria snatched it from her. 'I'll take that.' She said. 'Or, I'll no doubt have to make this journey alone anyway. You're more likely to roast yourself alive, than you are to lead us safely up the mountain. Besides, my body is designed to withstand heat. These flowers burn white hot; the heat around it will most likely melt the flesh clean off your bones.

Ohmiya smiled. 'You do care.' She said.

Soria laughed. 'I'm just getting used to you that's all. I would hate to see you die of your own stupidity.' She replied.

Ohmiya smiled again. 'I knew you cared more than you let on. And, now I know for sure.' She said.

Soria scoffed and walked past her. 'Let's get a move on! You said that we weren't far away now. So, how far is not far away?' she asked.

Ohmiya ran to catch up with Soria, who had begun to walk at a much faster pace now that she had the correct footwear. 'It should be just around the corner, just up ahead.' she said.

The night was drawing to a close. Both Snowflake and Mr. Fuzzy lay lifeless, only a few metres apart and in front of the cave's entrance in Glacia. Whatever magic had brought them together, had left them unconscious on the floor. Mr. Fuzzy was no longer a burning red, his colour had nearly faded and he had not moved since he arrived. Snowflake, too, was out cold. He had lost his sparkly coating and was almost invisible against the snow. The slush they were laid in had turned to ice, thus gluing them to the ground.

Although hard to see in the dimming sun, their scents carried for miles. It had attracted the attention of some smaller predators, but they couldn't get close enough to their prey. Yeti roamed around the two companions, yet they were oblivious to their presence. They were camouflaged, unseen and unheard, as the large white monsters fought over the leftovers of a deer. Two of the yeti pulled it apart like a wish bone, while the other was pushed away. He was smaller than the other's and would be lucky if he was allowed to lick the bones after they had finished. It slumped itself against the side of the cave and dozed off.   The other two, after finishing their evening snack, fell to the ground with a thud and blocked the entrance.

Ohmiya grabbed Soria's arm and pulled her back. 'Ouch! I told you to stop that.' She yelped.

Ohmiya held her finger pressed against her lips and shushed Soria. 'Don't you shush me.' She said.

Ohmiya put her hand over her mouth to stop her from barking at her anymore. 'Do you want to die? Because if not, I suggest you shut that mouth of yours and listen to what I have to say. Did you not hear that?' Ohmiya asked.

Soria gestured for Ohmiya to remove her hand from her face. 'Thank you. I cannot speak with your mitts on my mouth. Hear what, that banging noise?'

'Yes. It could be something we don't want to bump into. It sounded close.' Ohmiya said. 'We need to stay quiet from here on out.'

Soria smiled gleefully. 'You mean, I don't get to answer any more of your interesting, not remotely boring, questions? Oh drat, and I was so looking forward to the next part of the quiz.'

Ohmiya rolled her eyes. 'There is nothing wrong with my questions. But, yes, we have to stay quiet. At least until we get into the cave. It should be a few hundred feet that way. Snowflake and I were just there when I got zapped back halfway home again. So, with any luck, he will be sat there waiting for me to return, hopefully unharmed. And, I'm guessing, because you somehow ended up with me, Mr. Fuzzy could have ended up with Snowflake.' She said.

'Is that your expert opinion?' Soria asked sarcastically.

Ohmiya pulled at her poorly arm. 'Ouch! You said that you wouldn't do that again.' Said Soria angrily.

Ohmiya crossed her arms and raised an eyebrow. 'And, you said that you wouldn't behave the way you are doing anymore.' She replied.

Soria rubbed her arm. 'In my defence, I don't remember saying anything like that. But, your right. It is the only rational explanation, in this otherwise bazaar experience. I'll follow your lead.'

Ohmiya gestured for Soria to go ahead. 'No, it's okay, I'll let you lead. Besides, you have the torch remember. So, it makes sense for you to go first.'

Soria continued ahead and began to chunter. 'Oh, I see, I'm okay to lead now that we may be eaten, or disembowelled. That's it, put the bait out in front and make sure you have a fighting chance at running away.'

Ohmiya laughed at her rants. 'Just keep moving.' She said. 'It's just up ahead. I can see the clearing.'

Soria continued to walk and everything was quiet. Ohmiya didn't utter a word and followed closely behind. It was so quiet, that all they could hear was the squelching of the mammoth hide boots.

Ohmiya pointed ahead. 'There it is, just through those trees.' She whispered.

Soria called upon every ounce of energy she had left and began to run as fast as she could. She was almost at the clearing, when Ohmiya tackled her to the floor. Soria let go of the Etherflame and it went flying into the opening and landed on the floor. She put her hands over Soria's mouth and held her firmly down on the ground. 'I know that you probably want to hit me really hard for that, but trust me when I tell you not to make a sound.' She whispered in a deep commanding tone. 'I'm going to let go of you now. But, if you say anything louder than a whisper, then we are both yeti chowder. Do you understand?'

Soria, flabbergasted by her strength, nodded in agreement. Ohmiya released her grip and slowly backed off of her. 'Where?' asked Soria. 'Where are they?'

Ohmiya pointed out the three yeti that lay in an awkward pile in front of the entrance to the cave. They may have been big, but their coats were whiter than white, and they looked like heaped snow piles while asleep. 'You would not have seen them had I not pointed them out. I didn't know for sure they were here, but as I was chasing you up the hill, the smell of them became stronger. I knew they were close. Lucky for us, they are sleeping. Probably just finished eating. It's all they do: eat, fight and sleep.' She said.

Soria looked sick. 'Just eaten? Didn't you say Snowflake was supposed to be here, with Mr. Fuzzy? You don't think? Do you?' asked Soria.

Ohmiya realised what she had said and her eyes widened and began to dart back and forth with worry. The light of the Etherflame flickered in the opening before the cave. It burned bright, even against the snowy surface. Fortunately, it had not roused the monsters, and they continued to snore.

Soria looked at Ohmiya for a suggestion. 'Well, what now?' she asked. 'Where could they be, if not here? I refuse to believe they have been eaten. They're still alive, I can feel it.'

Ohmiya was equally hopeful. She continued to scout the area, but couldn't see her companion. Soria tugged at her arm. 'I think I see something.' She said.

'Where?' Ohmiya replied.

Soria pointed to what appeared to be a ball of fluff sticking out of the ground. 'There.' She said.

Ohmiya grinned. 'I see it.' She whispered. 'And there is another object there. Can you see?'

Soria smiled at the site of the burnt orange fur poking out of the ground. It had faded, and he was no longer glowing, but it was unmistakably him. The only colours she had seen since she had arrived in Glacia, were deep greens and bright whites; that fur coat could only have belonged to one other. Soria struggled to contain her excitement. 'Mr. Fuzzy!' she shouted.

Ohmiya tackled her to the floor and covered her mouth again. The yeti began to stir, but they did not wake. They were lucky. 'What did I say.' Ohmiya whispered loudly.

Soria snatched her hand from her mouth. 'I'm sorry, but he's there, and he's not getting up. He must be hurt. I need to get to him.' She pleaded.

Ohmiya pointed out to the other bump in the snow. 'And that, I think, is Snowflake over there. What is the point in us charging out there and getting eaten? That will help no one. They don't usually fall asleep in front of such an easy meal. My guess is that they haven't seen them yet. He obviously can't hear you, so something must have happened to them. But, if we are going to get them safely, we need a plan.' She said.

'What do you suggest?' asked Soria.

Ohmiya placed her forefinger and thumb under her chin and had begun to hatch a plan. She could not see an easy solution. If they charged out head on and grabbed their companions, it would rouse the yeti and they would not outrun them. Nor could they fight them, as they were impossibly outmatched. 'I know.' She said. 'Can you carry Mr. Fuzzy under that poorly arm of yours?'

Soria looked perplexed. 'I think so. Why?' She asked.

Ohmiya did not give out much information about the plan. She just gave a few instructions. 'When the time is right, you will run, grab our companions and get into the cave as quickly as possible.' She said.

Soria looked concerned. But, for the first time, she was not just concerned for her own safety. She was genuinely worried about

Ohmiya. 'And what will you do? How do you intend to get them to move?'

Ohmiya smiled. 'I was always wandering off as a youngling. I used to spend many hours watching the wild creatures of Glacia. Sometimes from the watchtowers within our city's walls. Sometimes I got up close. Anyway, the point is, I used to listen to the way they communicated with one another. I became quite good at mimicking them; in particular the ox and deer.'

Soria still looked confused. 'So?' she said.

'They are the yeti's favourite food. All I need to do, is get far enough away from here, but not so far they can't hear me. Then I make the noises as loudly as I can. Then, when they come after me, you can make a break for it. It couldn't be simpler.' She said proudly.

Soria raised an eyebrow. 'That is the stupidest thing I have ever heard.' She said. 'You will get yourself killed, and I, will no doubt have to look after two useless companions. It's hard enough taking care of one on my own.' She ridiculed.

'I knew you cared. I will be fine I promise.' She said, and began to run off in the opposite direction.

Soria tried to call her back, but she had already run off. She cussed her under her breath for leaving her alone. Now she had no choice but to play along with the plan she thought was lunacy. *How on earth does she plan to get away from them when they catch up to her, and realise that she isn't really an animal? What will she do them? Stupid girl is going to get herself killed.* She thought.

Soria watched as the brutes that blocked the way snored. Their stench was beginning to burn her nostrils. It was so vile she could taste their aroma; a mixture of sweat, rotting elk and faeces. One of them sneezed. Moist mist made it as far as where Soria was laid in the snow. It covered the ground in a moss green paste, and she started to wretch. It was, without a doubt, the most disgusting thing she had witnessed. 'What is taking so long?' She murmured under her breath.

She waited for several minutes, which felt like a great deal longer. Then, she heard it. Faint noises in the distance that sounded remarkably like animals. So much so, that she was unsure if they were coming from Ohmiya, or if they were indeed coming from the creatures she was trying to mimic.

The ears of the yeti who laid alone, the smallest one, who was a little farther away from the larger two, had begun to twitch. It started to move with its eyes still shut. Then they opened widely, and the whites of its eyes were yellowed and bloodshot. Its tusk-like teeth protruded from its mouth, when it smiled a vicious smile. When it stood, it was as tall as the nearby trees. The others began to rouse gradually, as Ohmiya continued to make the noises from afar. The smallest of the three started for the forest, but was tripped purposefully by one of the larger two. They then proceeded on before it. It got up angrily and followed them through the ferns.

Soria stood, but cautiously waited until she knew they had left. She ran over to the Etherflame first and picked it up from the snow. Then, she ran over to Mr. Fuzzy who was still knocked out. 'Come on little guy. Get up for me.' She pleaded for him to move. But it was no use. He was half frozen and stuck tight in the ground.

She tried to crack the ground around him and dig him out. But the ground was too tough. The solid ice split her knuckles as she punched the floor. Then, she had a thought. She placed the Etherflame to the ice. It began to melt rapidly and she was able to pull him free. She pulled him close to her chest and cuddled him for a little while. 'I'm sorry.' She said. 'I'm sorry I was so mean to you before. It's only because it was the only way I knew. I promise I'll be better from now on. Please. Please wake up.' She stroked his fur and had begun to cry. She did not often cry. She always believed that showing her emotions was a sign of weakness. But she realised in that moment, that her anger was an emotion too. An emotion that had caused her more harm than good. She was always angry, always on guard. She never allowed herself to be vulnerable. But she could not deny herself the feeling of sadness any longer. She sobbed hard, whilst she was holding her companion. The pain of losing him was as unbearable as losing Solis. She rubbed his fur to warm him up. She squeezed him tight and kept asking him to wake up.

194

Just when she had nearly given up hope, just when she thought she had lost him for good, he began to move. His fur became a little brighter and his body had begun to warm. He did not open his eyes, but he opened his mouth widely and gave her his signature smile.

Soria smiled back and cried harder. 'I can't believe you did that to me. Don't you ever do that to me again. I can't lose you too.' She wept. 'Come on anyway. Tender as this moment may be, we have to save another. Come on.'

She lifted him from the floor and carried him over to Snowflake. She used the Etherflame to melt the ice around his body, yet she did not hold it too close. Mr. Fuzzy, was able to withstand the heat like she could, but the flame could well have burnt Snowflake to a cinder. The ice loosened and she pulled him free. He was moving, albeit slowly. The ice must not have bothered him the same way that it had Mr. Fuzzy. Nonetheless, he was weak. She needed to take him to safety. So, she picked him up and placed him under her other arm, and made her way to the cave's entrance. It was impossibly black, and almost identical to the cavern's entrance in Athia. Luckily, the Etherflame was still alight and she was able to see the way ahead.

She perched herself behind a large rock in the entrance and sat waiting. Waiting patiently for her friend to return. *Come on Ohmiya. Don't you dare leave me here alone,* She thought.

It had been half an hour since Ohmiya ran into the forest. The noises she made had stopped quite some time ago, and the night-time had crept in. *She was right,* thought Soria, *it really is dark on a night here. Not even the stars are as bright as they are in Athia.* Her mind wandered as she gazed into the night. She wondered if the stars were even the same here as they were at home. Although it was believed that the Sapphire Stream was no more than a few miles across, it always seemed like worlds away to the Athianne; Glacia, as Soria now knew it to be, was as much a story as the tale of the two dragons. It was known to exist, as the world was not believed to reach its end at the Sapphire Stream, but it could never have been described.

There may not have been much light in the night, but what little light there was, gave off a dazzling display. The ground glittered in the presence of the moon. It shone through ice that formed on the trees, which sparkled like twinkling lights on the tips of the branches.

She thought of Ohmiya, and how her hair also sparkled. She hadn't realised she had paid that much attention, but she had. She thought about how she would love to be asked another question. And, as infuriating as they may have been at the time, it was preferable to the deafening silence of the empty cave; or, at least she had hoped that it was empty. She was in no state to defend herself, as her arm could barely carry the extremely light weight of Snowflake.

She released him gently onto the ground and rubbed his coarse fur with the back of her hand. The furry barbs scratched her hand. *I can't believe how much alike you are to my companion,* she thought, as she looked at Mr. Fuzzy, *the resemblance is uncanny. Yet you are, in a way, completely different.* Then, she stroked the softer fur coat of her own companion, and they both smiled adoringly at one another.

'I think he'll be okay here a minute. Shall we see if we can see her coming back?' she asked Mr. Fuzzy. But, as he always did, her companion smiled gormlessly and stuck out his tongue. Soria acknowledged Mr. Fuzzy's smile, as though she could tell what he was thinking. 'That's what I thought.' She said, and picked up the Etherflame, that was still burning assiduously, and crept quietly out of the entrance.

She waved the blazing torch left and right, but could see no further than a few metres ahead. The arctic breeze nipped her knees, cheeks and fingertips, as they were the only parts of her body still showing. She could bear it no longer, so she went back into the cave to escape the wind's wrath.

She waited a further five minutes, and Ohmiya hadn't returned. Fearing the worst, she looked deeper into the cave. She did not want to go in alone, but she did not fancy her chances against Glacia alone. She thought of the horror stories she was told as a youngling, about ferocious beasts; about how they would attack unsuspecting victims and carry them away in the night. She thought about how the other children would quiver in fear at the mere idea of them, whereas she would remain unaffected. The very notion of anything so ferocious existing, thrilled her, and excited her. She wondered how she could have been so cavalier.

Maybe it's because they were only stories, she pondered, *and maybe on some level I never believed they ever truly existed. But, now; now I am living the life I longed for as a youngling, and now I am surrounded by real horrors, real creatures that would happily use my bones for toothpicks after devouring me. Maybe that's why I feel so scared right now. Because, this is real life. It is easy to say how you would act in the face of something you never truly expect to encounter. It is not so easy to act as you said you would, when the time actually arises.*

Soria had begun to realise, that the scariest thing about Glacia, was not the beasts that lurked in the night. It was not the fact that she was alone. It was the realisation, that she had not met any of her prior expectations. She had thought so highly of herself for so long, that she failed to see any of her own flaws. With no real threat to contemplate in Athia, for the longest time, she had professed to be fearless, professed to be strong and ruthless. But, it was easy to be fearless, when there was nothing to fear. However, Glacia had given her the opportunity to experience fear, and what's more, the opportunity to overcome it.

She took one last look behind her into the cave, to decide whether or not to go it alone. Then, she turned back out towards the exit, to see if she could see Ohmiya. As she turned back, a figure jumped out from her left. 'Boo!' Ohmiya shouted.

Soria leapt into the air and landed back on her feet like a startled cat. She stormed over to Ohmiya like a rabid dog, and Ohmiya shielded herself. She thought that Soria was about to strike her, but instead, she wrapped her arms around her tightly.

'I half expected you to hit me.' Said Ohmiya. 'I didn't expect this. Not from you anyway. Did you hit your head or something?'

Soria let go of her and Ohmiya let out a gasp in jest, pretending that she had been held so tight that she could no longer breathe. 'Joke all you will. Honestly, though, I am glad you're okay. Who else would I have to irritate me until I get home?' Soria asked rhetorically.

The two girls smiled at each other. Soria felt warm in her presence, even in the harsh nights air. 'How did you get away?' Soria asked.

Ohmiya laughed aloud. 'Well, I just called them over, then hid in this big tree. Those yeti are scary strong, but not so much with the brains.' She twirled her fingers near her temples.

But, as Ohmiya was talking, 'Watch out!' shouted Soria, then pushed Ohmiya out of the way. A yeti came charging through the trees swinging its arms clumsily at Soria. She flew through the air and landed several feet away in the snow. Ohmiya pulled herself up and saw it walking towards Soria, who was still face down in the snow. She picked up the blazing flower a little too close to the fiery end, which burnt her hand, and charged at the beast with it. She waved it swiftly side to side, which left trails in the air where it had been. She made patterns in the air and lashed at the yeti with the flame. It looked confused, then backed off from her.

Soria rose from the snow and called out to her. 'Behind you.' She yelled. But it was too late, the other yetis had also caught up to her. As the wind was drifting down the mountain, so too had the yeti's smell, and she was unaware that they had followed her back.

One of them grabbed her by the leg, while the other one poked at her. She dangled in the air, with no hope of escape. 'Let her go!' Begged Soria, who was also lifted into the air by her arm; her bruised arm.

Both girls cried out for help. They swayed themselves trying to break free. This seemed to please the yeti, who were known for toying with their food, so they let them keep calling out for help. Just as the smallest yeti, the one that had hold of Soria, was about to begin his feast, a bright light luminated the place. The air grew warmer, then hotter. The snow on the floor had begun to melt and the breeze had dipped. Mr. Fuzzy was glowing again. Just like he had in the cavern, only this time, he wasn't just glowing, he was burning. Flames flashed from his fur like solar flares, and he looked like a miniature sun. He was not smiling; for one of only a few times since he came to being, he was not smiling. Looking like he could spontaneously combust, the angry little fireball ran headfirst at the yeti that held his keeper. He rammed into the side of its leg and it set its fur alight. The yeti hopped around making loud pitched screams, then let go of Soria, and had begun to slap it's leg to put the fire out. The stubborn fire persisted to work its way up the yeti, and it's hand caught fire. It ran off into the forest and never came back.

The yeti that held Ohmiya seemed unconcerned. It laughed as its friend caught fire and continued to taunt her by swinging her back and forth. It swung her high in the air then opened it's disgusting mouth. Ohmiya was freefalling into its jaws when another bright light emanated from the cave entrance; it was electric blue. This stunned the remaining two yeti, and Ohmiya fell face down in the frozen snow. Snowflake emerged from the cave, alive and illuminated. His coarse fur was stood on end, like a bright blue porcupine. It saw its keeper and the two-rampaging beasts beside her. It ran, although no one knows how it moved so quick, and jumped into the air. It exploded like a puffer fish, and fired out its barb pine fur at the yeti. The pines struck the monsters like an automatic nail gun and they ran for the hills.

Soria pulled Ohmiya to her feet and both girls looked at their companions. The red and blue balls of light began to dim. They no longer looked angry, and returned to their usual states. Both girls picked up their companions and looked at one another, mystified.

'Well.' Soria started. 'That was unexpected.' Ohmiya continued. 'It was interesting.' Soria finished.

The light had not completely vanished, and both Snowflake and Mr. Fuzzy continued to give off a faint glow. They looked different to what they did before, as though being near one another, brought forth something that laid dormant within them. The red and blue pulsated simultaneously. Snowflake was ice cold to touch, and Mr. Fuzzy felt like a naked flame. Yet, in the hands of their keepers, they were completely harmless.

'I guess you're not so useless after all.' Said Soria remorsefully, as though she was taking back twelve years of hate with one apology.

Ohmiya laughed. 'They never were.' She said. 'They just needed a reason to show us what they could really do. Sometimes it takes something drastic to change someone. I'm guessing that was the first time you had ever hugged someone.'

Soria laughed. 'Ha. Yeah, but don't get used to it. I thought you had been eaten, and that I was going to have to make the rest of the journey alone. I was just checking to see if you were real, and that I wasn't hallucinating. Besides, now I know that Mr. Fuzzy is like a walking volcano, I don't even think I need you anymore.' She said.

Ohmiya started to walk into the cave with a deep grin on her face. 'You can't go on without me, face it, we are joined at the hip from now on and there is nothing you can do about it. And, it was a real hug, even if you don't want to admit it; it's fine, I know the truth.'

Soria picked up the Etherflame from the floor. She pulled another from out of her backpack and set it alight with the other. 'Here.' She said. 'Take this, in case we do get separated again. You probably won't be able to see without it.'

Ohmiya reached out for the Etherflame, but then pulled her hand back. Her hand had already blistered from picking it up before. 'Just don't grab the end that's alight this time, and it will be fine. The stalk is longer on this one.' Said Soria.

'Okay, thank you.' And she took the flower from Soria gratefully. It felt warm against her skin, but as Soria had promised, it did not burn her.

Chapter Thirteen

A rgon bent low. The ground was stained red; not the rusty red of the Athianne plains, but the colour of freshly spilled blood. He touched it and rubbed it between his forefinger and thumb, *still warm,* he thought, *and still wet.* He looked further ahead, and could see the trail of blood led behind a small bush. The leaves were stained with the same red and he could hear a whimpering. He crept, quiet as a mouse, and peered behind the bushes. There was a fox, laid on its side, lifeless, and another licking its fur in hopes of reviving it. 'What has happened here little fella.' Said Argon, to the whimpering mate of the dead fox. It did not run away; instead it stroked itself up against Argon for comfort. He stroked it delicately and it sat at his feet. He knelt down and turned over the dead animal to look at its wound. He felt instantly nervous, his head flicked right then left like a meerkat. His heart had begun to pound like a beating drum and his hands had begun to shake. 'What could have done this to you, you poor little thing?' he turned to the fox. 'What on earth did this?' the fox licked its paw and had begun to preen itself. 'I don't know why I expected an answer from you. It's a shame you can't speak. I have never seen anything like this before. What could have made such a fatal wound?' he said to himself.

He placed his fingers in his mouth and whistled, although a human would not have been able to hear it, it could carry through the air to his companion. He called the phoenix to warn Aylen of potential danger ahead. He had mastered the art of speaking through whistle to his clever companion. It had never been useful for anything other than locating berries and other foods before. Never had he needed to warn anyone of danger. But in that moment, he was glad it was something he taken the time to teach her.

He looked again at the wound. Half of the fox was missing, and an Athianne fox was not as small as a regular fox. They were as large as a large domestic dog, so whatever had bitten into it, must have been very large. He studied the teeth marks. The blood was hard at the entry marks, as though the teeth had instantly cauterised the flesh when they pierced it. *I don't know what made this bite mark, but I sure as hell don't want to meet the mouth that made it,* he thought.

Aylen and Torch had travelled up to the mountains' base; they had made it there in no time at all. They did not climb to the top of the first peak. Torch seemed startled and stopped dead in his tracks. He bucked like a wild bull on the spot and Aylen had to cling on for dear life. 'Calm down Torch, what is it? What is it?' she stroked behind his ears and whispered calming words to him.

He eventually calmed and began to sniff the floor. His ears pointed up and twisted in all directions like the neck of an owl. His fur coat began to glow and emit a scorching heat. He growled deeply and gazed back towards the village. Aylen had not needed to instruct him to turn back. He did so without command and set off back. Aylen had no control over her blazing companion. He howled into the night and Argon's phoenix lit the sky like a fire work display. *What is going on? Why won't you listen to me boy? What is Argon's companion doing here without him?* Aylen deliberated. No matter how hard she tried, she could not get Torch to stop. So she resigned herself to the fact that they were going wherever he was leading them to, and she would have no choice but to hold on for the ride.

Argon's companion was a bird on fire. He led the way, crying mightily like an eagle on the hunt. *Maybe he has picked up on Soria's sent, and perhaps… perhaps she truly is in danger. Maybe Argon is too, and that is why his companion has come to warn us. I wonder if that is why Torch is so riled,* she pondered.

Aylen felt guilty about her last words to Soria. She had hated her for years, yet she also respected her. Aylen, although contained within a guise of supremacy, and liked to flaunt her prowess, was still the same timid girl she had always been within. Though she would never admit it, she would have been scared by her own shadow, had it not been for her companion. What had slipped her attention was the floor that had been dusted with freshly formed tracks from the feet of a hoard of lycunflame. Torch had picked up the scent and was racing frantically to catch up to them, as they were heading back in the direction of the village.

***

The ground had begun to shake irrepressibly. It ripped through Glacia without remorse, taking down trees, trapping wildlife and battering the landscape. The Glacianne struggled to stand behind their walls as the ground shook. The spires that held the fort together began to split. They fell through the floor as the ground opened and swallowed them up. Freya ordered those who guarded the wall to fall back. Some met an unfortunate end as they slipped through the cracks in the floor and were crushed under the wall that once protected them. Others watched hopelessly as their friends and family were lost under the devastation.

The cries were heard by the creatures that waited patiently for a weak point to appear. One lone wolf jumped over the gap in the floor and breached the cities defences. Hunters surrounded the beast, but it was ravenous and ready to pounce. It attacked a woman, who managed to hold it back with the handle of her spear. Freya charged through the chaos picked up a spear from a fallen hunter, then launched it precisely at the wolf. It hit the beast so hard, that it went soaring through the air and landed in the crevice made by the quake. 'Everyone guard the gap!' she bellowed. 'One made it across and others will follow.'

The woman who was about to be torn apart, still laid flat on the floor, thanked Freya as she gave her a hand to her feet. 'Don't thank me just yet Astrid. This is just the start. There is still a chance that we may not make it out of this alive.'

Astrid, who was shaking, was confused at her orders. 'What are we waiting for Freya? Why are we not retreating? This place is not safe anymore. We need to leave while we still can. What are we waiting for?' she asked.

Freya dug deep within herself for the strength to enforce her decision to stay. She had to believe it was the right move, in order to convince the others it was the right move. With the chief dead, his wife indisposed, and the newly appointed chieftainess nowhere to be seen, morale was low. 'We are staying, because this has been our home for generations. We cannot abandon it now. We must defend our right to be here. If we leave now, where would we go? Leaving will only make us more vulnerable. We will be picked off one at a time in the forest. We cannot hope to run away in the night when we are at our weakest. We must stay and defend ourselves, and show them our strength. They will give up when they see us fight back. They are mindless creatures who can smell our fear. We must show them we are not afraid, and this is a meal that will not be easily attained. When they realise that we are not ripe for the picking, they will abandon their campaign.' She affirmed her speech with an authoritive nod.

'That's all well and good. But, what about the next night, and the next night.' She replied concerned. 'If our city falls, we cannot rebuild it in a day. They will come back. What then?' asked Astrid.

Freya shared her concern, but was focused on the now. She also placed a great deal of faith in young Ohmiya. 'Ohmiya, is currently on a quest to seek out the white dragon. Our chieftainess will have the answer on her return.' She said.

Astrid looked sceptical. 'And, what if she doesn't return? It is not a journey anyone has ever made. We don't even know if the dragon exists. What if the stories are false? We can't surely be putting all our faith in the hands of a girl and a myth?' she asked.

Freya looked down on Astrid angrily. 'Had I known I was saving someone with such a revolting mind, I mightn't have saved you. Ohmiya will return. And what's more, she will have the resolution to the problem. And, do not ever question the existence of our guardian again. Unsavoury thoughts such as those may be the reason for the falling of our city's walls. If we no longer believe in our guardian, maybe he no longer believes we deserve his protection. Therefore, it is vital that one of us revitalises that belief. Ohmiya will succeed at this task.' She pointed at the hole in the city's walls. 'Now, Astrid, get into position. Ready the rest of the hunters for an imminent attack.' Freya ordered.

Astrid obeyed and saluted Freya in response. Freya was still split. On the surface she was holding it together, but inside she feared for Ohmiya. *I pray you get back to us soon little one. We need a miracle if we are to survive this. The fate of our people rests in your hands.*

***

The cave was impossibly black, except for the light emitted from the flames of the Etherflame flowers. Ohmiya, had seemingly forgotten about the close encounter with the yetis, as she skipped through the glacial cavern with excitement. The walls were frozen solid, and seemed to expand the further in they wandered. Her fingers glided across the glittery surface, as she stroked the walls whilst walking. The ceiling was too high to touch, too high to see. 'I wonder how far in it goes?' she pondered aloud.

Soria scouted for danger. It was not the first time she had ventured into a cave and wished she hadn't. While Ohmiya danced around like an ignorant child, with wonder in her eyes, Soria stayed cautious of their surroundings. 'Maybe we ought to slow down a little bit. I trusted you to lead us in the right direction out there, but in here, neither of us know where we are going.'

Ohmiya laughed. 'There is only one way. Straight forward.' She replied, and continued to skipped through the cave, followed closely by her companion, who waddled behind her at a hasty pace.

'I thought that the white dragon would live at the top in the third cave. That's how the story goes, is it not?' asked Soria.

Ohmiya laughed again. 'No, that is the red dragon, *"highest peak of the tallest mountain…"*, is that not how the story goes? ' she said. 'Here, there maybe three main entrances to the cave, but they all lead to the same place. The one at the top is just a bigger entrance. Can you imagine a dragon as large as our guardian fitting through that tiny entrance we just walked through?'

Soria mumbled something under her breath and raised an eyebrow cynically. 'Be that as it may, I still think we should slow down. We don't know what horrors wait for us ahead.' She said.

An echo came back from within, as Ohmiya had run off faster than Soria could keep up. 'All the horrors are outside; we are safe in here. No one enters these caves.'

Soria mumbled under her breath again. 'Or, is it just that no one comes out to tell the tale?'

They had walked for an hour, until the walls were as far apart as the ceiling was from the floor. The temperature declined rapidly and a slow breeze flowed through the cave. It's chill reached Soria's bones and made her shudder. Ohmiya, too, felt the cold, but it did not stop her moving forward. She was still a little ahead and all that could be seen by Soria was the faint flicker of the flame around a sharp corner. 'Come quick!' Shouted Ohmiya from ahead. 'Come here quickly, you've got to see this!'

She ran to catch her up and skidded around the corner on the frictionless floor. The Etherflame was dropped to the floor, and her jaw dropped as she gawked upward. Moonlight filtered in through a giant hole in the ceiling, and shone down on a diamond wall, that was as far wide as it was high. It shone with the strength of a thousand stars and hurt her eyes as they re-adjusted.

'Wow, it's incredible. I've never seen anything like it.' Said Soria in awe. She walked up to Ohmiya, who was stood by it.

Ohmiya looked sad. 'I have…' She said. 'It's the same material used in the walls of our city. The city that is currently crumbling.'

Soria looked confused. 'That's great.' Said Soria. 'Isn't it? There must be enough material here to rebuild a thousand city's.'

Ohmiya still looked sad. 'No, not a thousand.' She replied. 'There's enough for just one.'

Soria still looked confused, as she looked at a seemingly limitless diamond supply. 'I don't understand. Besides, I thought we were going to seek out the white dragon. He can help you, and me, remember? We just need to keep moving.'

'You don't understand. There is no further to go. All directions now lead back out of the cave. Don't ask me how I know that, it's just a feeling.' She replied and had started to cry.

Soria became cross with her. 'Stop that now. That can't be right, or the stories are false, and what we have been told is a lie. I don't believe that our entire people's lives are built on a lie. I refuse to believe that. Because if the white dragon doesn't exist, then neither does the red dragon. It can't be true. He has to be here somewhere. We will find him.' She grabbed Ohmiya by the arm and pulled her away, as she wept by the wall.

Ohmiya shrugged her off and pushed her back. 'You don't get it. That is how I know that there is no further we can go, and there is nowhere else to look. He is here!' She shouted at her.

'What are you talking about? Have you gone crazy in this cave?' She twirled her finger by her temple to insinuate she was going mad. 'Where is he then? Where is he if he is here, because I don't see him anywhere?'

Ohmiya pointed to the diamond wall. 'He is here; are you blind? Our city was a gift from the white dragon. His skin forms the very walls of our home.'

Soria laughed with hysteria. 'You can't be serious. This wall must be at least two hundred feet tall, and it goes all the way around to the other side of the room. Plus, it doesn't even look like a dragon; does it? Where is its face, or its feet? It's just an extremely large, rock-hard chunk of diamond.' She said.

Ohmiya did not answer her. She was drifting in and out of a daydream. She was thinking about what to do next.

Soria pleaded with her to snap out of it, 'What are you doing, we can't stop now, we can't give up now. What about me, what about my people? It's not all about you!' She said.

Ohmiya was fuming, so she pushed her away. 'All about me?' She screamed at Soria, then prodded her sharply with her finger. 'That's rich coming from you! All you care about is yourself. Poor little Soria, needing recognition and to prove how strong you are.'

She said mockingly, the continued to shout. 'At least I'm not making this journey to resolve my own internal issues! At least I'm not doing this for selfish reasons! You're just egotistical and full of childish need! Just go! Just leave me alone!'

Soria was hurt. It wasn't the first time she had been told the truth about herself. But, it was the first time she had been told by someone she cared about. Aylen upset her, but Ohmiya's words cut deep. 'You are right.' She replied. 'Every word of it. I am selfish. I did set out on this journey for reasons that weren't entirely selfless. Although I wanted to help the people of Athia, I guess what I really wanted was to prove my worth.'

Ohmiya pouted. 'At least you admit it. I guess that makes a change.' She said.

Soria placed her hand on Ohmiya's shoulder. 'I have changed, though, can't you see that? Or, at least, I'm starting to. I may have started on this journey for myself. But when I met you only a short time ago now, all that started to change. The old me would have just walked away from you. The old me wouldn't have cared about anyone else's problems. And, maybe at first, I didn't really care about your problems, or you. But, after a short time with you, I started to care about you, I started to care about my friend. And that seems strange coming out of my mouth, because I never really cared about anyone other than myself before. Because I never really had a friend before. Then, after I saved you and we ended up stuck together for reasons unknown...' Ohmiya interrupted. 'I saved you, I think, but go on. I like where this is leading...' Soria continued. 'We can agree to disagree on that one. But anyway, I went from being stuck with you, to realising I wanted to be around you. This quest, if we can call it that, became less about my problems, and more about me helping you with yours. I wanted to help you. I wanted to help my friend. And, the truth is, I can't do this without you. And, I know if I left now, you wouldn't be able to do this without me either.'

Ohmiya smiled. 'Wow, you have changed. You've gotten soft. I don't think I like you like this. I think I preferred you a little more hard faced.' She said, and wiped the tears from her watering eyes.

Soria looked irritated, crossed her arms and turned away from her sharply. 'Well, don't get used to it. This is the one and only time I will apologise. Take it, or leave it.'

Ohmiya wrapped her arms around her. 'Apology accepted.' She said.

Soria turned to face her, and both girls smiled at each other. Soria held out her hand, 'Friends?' she asked.

Ohmiya grabbed her hand and shook it extatically. 'Definitely.' She said.

'So, this big chunk of shiny rock is the dragon then? I thought he would be a bit more, what's the word, dragony?' asked Soria.

Ohmiya laughed. 'That's not even a word.'

'I'm sure it is.' Said Soria. 'Or, if it isn't, it should be.'

Ohmiya looked up at the diamond scales. 'I see what you mean, though, he isn't as impressive as I thought he would be.' And both girls continued to discuss what to do next.

As they were chattering, they hadn't noticed the diamond scales had begun to change shape. A large portion of the structure began to move. It was the shape of a tail and it coiled around them slowly in a serpent like motion. Two large, electric blue eyes opened and stared down on them. A large gust of wind swept past them, when a large pair of nostrils flared to take a breath, then soaked them in an icy cold dew as it exhaled.

A deep deafening voice shook the walls as it spoke. 'Well, I was beginning to worry you two would never show up.' It said.

Both girls turned to face the wall with astonishment. The chunk of diamond in the centre of the room began to unwind like a spring and open out. They were frozen, from both the icy cold breath that beat down on them, and in fear. One large wing sprang out and filled the room, or at least what remained of the room, which was not already filled with the enormity of the white dragon.

Soria was the first to speak. 'You're the white dragon?' she said, and Ohmiya gawked at her with scrutiny. *What a positively ridiculous statement,* she thought, *of course it's the flaming white dragon.*

The dragon was less bothered by her obvious statement, and graced her with an answer anyway. 'I am my child.' He said, and the room shook with every word he spoke.

'And you've been expecting us? How is that possible?' she asked a more appropriate question.

'I have known that we would meet for quite some time now, before I knew what the reason for our meeting would be.'

Ohmiya stepped forward. 'How is that possible? Did you know that we would eventually seek you out, that we would need your help?' she asked.

'I knew that you would seek me out, yes. But, the reason you are here, is not the reason you think.' He said, then panted as though he was struggling for breath.

Soria spoke less respectfully. 'We are not here to save you; we are here to find out why our homes are being destroyed. You are supposed to protect us. Why are Athia and Glacia falling apart?'

'Ah Soria, your temperament is as fiery as my brother's flame. To save your people, and to save the land you love, you must first save me. Both problems are one and the same.'

Ohmiya held Soria back and spoke calmly. 'Why do you need saving? Are you sick? Dying? And, if so, what can we do? Why us? Why not someone else, anyone else? We struggled to even reach you, as you didn't even see fit to bestow upon us stronger companions.' And, she gestured to Mr. Fuzzy and Snowflake who were attempting to lick their own eyeballs.

The white dragon laughed. 'Ha, no I am not sick. I am simply stuck. The earthquake that shook the lands, also shook the cave. I forged my home in this cave from my very own ice. And, large chunks of it fell from the walls and landed on my left wing and limbs. I am stuck to this spot and cannot move it. If I don't break free from here, I will starve and die. I needed someone to help free me. The weaker I grow, the warmer Athia and Glacia will become. When I am free, and my strength is restored, all will return to the way it once was.

'And, why you? Because you are the strongest of both your respective tribes. Who else could have braved the journey here during such trying times? The climate changing rapidly, the creatures of the land more ravenous and dangerous than ever, and your way of life on the brink of breaking down. You battled your way up here with courage, strength and will power. You did not need a companion to ride, or do your battles for you. You fought alongside them. And, in doing so, you brought out their true potential. And as for their strength; it exceeds that of any other.

They just needed the right keepers to bring it out of them. But, they are also stronger together. The further apart they are from one another, the weaker they become. They have only just begun to show you what they can do.'

Both girls listened intently, but were bursting with questions. Soria interrupted him, 'That's great, but it doesn't explain how we got here in the first place, or how we are to help you break free? If you can't lift away the rubble with all the strength you possess, how are we supposed to help you lift it?'

The white dragon answered her, 'You were teleported here by your companion. Both of your companions are connected in a way that you are yet to understand. They can teleport to one another; this can sometimes happen unwittingly when one is in immediate danger. And, they can also teleport you to where you need to be, if they have been there before. But, they can only do that when they are together. When they are separated, they can only teleport to one another. Like you and Ohmiya will grow to be, they are stronger together. And, as for the lifting of the rubble that pins me to this spot; I can lift a lesser weight, but there is too much for me alone. The ice from my breath can only be melted under the heat of my brother's flame. And, Mr. Fuzzy can burn with that very same heat. If he can melt away the majority of the ice on top of me, then I can lift away the rest of the rock. But he could not do what is needed without two things. Snowflake, to increase his power, and the love of his keeper. It is your love for Mr. Fuzzy, and his love for you, that has enabled him to become strong enough to burn so brightly. I can sense a great bond between the two of you, even if you cannot see it yourself.'

Soria spoke in a sarcastic tone. 'So, why didn't your brother, the red dragon, just fly over here and save you when you got stuck? Why wait for us? This all seems a little bit pointless.'

The white dragon laughed a deep laugh and spoke as candidly as the Athianne chieftainess. 'It is not your place to question our motives for what we do little one. We are not everlasting, nor are we all powerful. We can sense danger before it occurs, yes; sometimes years before. But, we do not always know what that danger is. Humans have relied on dragons for centuries: for protection, for help to prosper and for many other reasons. But, the relationship requires some give and take. So, it is not unreasonable for us to assume, that if we needed some help in return, that it would be offered willingly without question. It is necessary, from time to time, for us to test the strength of humankind, to see if you can rise to the challenge. And, you have risen most magnificently to this challenge.

'Also, it is not within our power to see whether something is wrong with the other. My brother may be sleeping soundly, seemingly unaware of the current state of affairs. I do not blame him for not coming to my aid, as he would not blame me for not coming to his, if I was unaware I was needed. It would take more than a simple earthquake to wake a dragon in slumber. And, it would seem, that a few large sheets of ice and boulders would do just that. If I had not had half of my home collapse in on me, I too would be sound asleep.' The white dragon coughed sickly, which broke him from his speech.

Ohmiya pleaded with her guardian for an answer to her current crisis.

He answered her sharply. 'First, release me from under this infernal heap of rock, then I will help you save your homes.'

The white dragon looked at Mr. Fuzzy, who looked less gormless than usual, and responded to the white dragons request without being asked. He could command him to do whatever he wished, as it was the dragons that breathed life into the magical creatures. Soria looked at Mr. Fuzzy as he ignited with the heat of a tiny sun, and hopped onto each large sheet of ice one at a time. They melted almost instantly. After several minutes, the floor was flooded with water and the two girls had had to hop onto the tail of the white dragon to escape the rising water. After a short while longer, all that remained of the rubble, was broken rock and debris from the caved in snow cave. The white dragon groaned with delight and thrust his wing in the air and stood on his hind legs. 'That's much better.' He said happily. 'Much better indeed. It may take a little while, but I will heal. It's nothing a few good meals and some well-earned rest won't cure. Maybe I'll have yeti for supper. Those three who caused you some trouble a little while ago will do nicely.'

'You saw that?' Ohmiya asked. 'How?'

The white dragon placed his front feet firmly on the floor and the whole ground shuddered under his unimaginable weight. 'I see all, my child. I could see as your precious city began to fall, and I could see the trouble you went through to reach me. It pained me to see everything and not be able to do anything. I could also see what happened in Athia, and what is about to happen if you do not return within the hour. However, now I am free, and it is I that owe you both a great debt, I can help you.'

Soria spoke with panic in her voice. 'What is about to happen in Athia?'

'The last earthquake may not have awoken my brother, but what it did release was a hoard of blood thirsty lycunflame. They managed to survive in the mountains where my brother sleeps, but, I dare say, they are instinctively attracted to the taste of Athianne. Even as we speak, they are heading towards your village. If you do not get to them in time, then I am afraid, there may be no one left to return to.'

Soria was horrified. She yanked at Ohmiya's arm and pleaded with her to move. The white dragon placed his tail across the entrance. 'What are you doing?' she cried; we need to go now.'

'You cannot hope to reach Athia on foot within the hour, as it will take longer than that to get out of this cave. The only way there is to teleport, with the help of your companions. But, you cannot hope to fight them alone. There are close to a hundred of them, and only two of you. You need an army to fight back.' He said

Ohmiya asked the white dragon, 'Where are we going to find an army to fight the lycunflame in Athia in such little time.'

The white dragon laughed. 'Are you not the chieftainess of the Glacianne tribe? Who, I believe, is in charge of some of the finest hunters around. They will do fine to fight against such a creature. And, the lycunflame may be deadly, but weapons forged from my own ice, cannot be melted under the heat of their flames. That right is reserved for only a select few. And, alas, it pains me to say it, but your people, Ohmiya, are, too, in great danger. They are currently surrounded by many creatures, who would very much like to have your people for dinner. But, I dare say, a little fire would scare them right off. You see, they have never seen fire before, and I am sure, that if Mr. Fuzzy here shows them what he can really do, they will not be bothering your people again in a hurry. Which will give your tribe the time it needs to repair its city. And I do believe, as luck would have it, I am due to shed my skin any day now. So as gift for your aid, I can restore your home to its former glory. And, for Soria's assistance, I am sure that your people would be more than happy to assist the Athianne with their current problem. So, it would seem, that all you have left to do, is return home. And, as I said before, I can help with this.'

Ohmiya and Soria looked at one another. 'Ready to save both our people?' said Ohmiya.

'I'm ready.' Soria replied. They both smiled at each other and their companions hopped onto their shoulders.

'What do we need to do?' they asked together.

'All you need to do.' Said the white dragon. 'Is think about where you wish to be taken, and it is vital that you are unanimous with your thoughts, then say aloud the place you wish to go.'

The two girls took a deep breath and nodded. They both thought solely of the Glacianne city. Although, as Soria had never seen it, she just repeated the word internally in the hope that it would work. Ohmiya thought hard of home, of her mother and of Freya. They took one last look at one another, then together, they said, 'The Glacianne City.'

Chapter Fourteen

T he fallen spires, that once formed the walls of the
Glacianne city, were being gathered by the yeti.
They were using them to build a bridge between the
gap that separated them from their meal. The tribe's hunters were
trying to push them back with little success. The yeti were too
strong; some held the bridge in place while others had begun to cross.
Freya's companion charged at them and howled powerfully. The yeti
held their hands to their ears and knelt down, as the wolf continued to
unleash a deafening noise. It then jumped at one and knocked it over

the side of the bridge and it plummeted into the gaping hole in the ground. Another tried to make its way across, so the wolf sunk its sharp teeth into the forearm of the beast. It swung its arm side to side, and as strong as the wolf was, it was forced to let go. The yeti thrashed around, then threw Freya's companion back into the city. It crashed into a pile of hunters like a set of skittles and knocked them to the ground.

A hoard of yeti crossed the makeshift bridge and breached the city's defences. Zorn, Ceyhan and the other watchers in the towers abandoned their posts to join the battle. Swarths of savage beasts entered the Glacianne city and had begun to herd the tribes folk like cattle. They were kept at bay, unable to attack, due to long sharpened spears held by the hunters and the companions protecting their keepers. Cornered, it was a battle of will and perseverance that would determine who would have been the victor. The Glacianne, frozen in fear, held formation, but dared not strike first; one wrong move could have been their undoing. And the creatures that surrounded them were all too aware of the sharp edges of the permafrost weaponry that faced them. They, too, dared not attack, as an injured animal was no less likely to be eaten than a human. It was a showdown of patience and resilience; who would tire first, or, who would give in first?

The Glacianne's companions were not built for war. Many were excellent hunting partners who could sniff out prey, that would otherwise elude their keeper. Some, like Freya's wolf, could take on the larger carnivores and keep her safe for a time. But, they were not large enough to battle against such a formidable foe. The Glacianne hunters companions were a collection of foxes, birds and small bears. Only Freya's wolf and the late chief's bear would have stood a chance against such a huge opposition. The late chief's companion watched over the vulnerable, while Freya tended to her injured companion, who was mortally wounded from his last fight.

Freya ripped a piece of her clothing and wrapped it tightly around her companion's injured leg like a bandage. It stained red instantly, as blood seeped through from the deep laceration to its front leg. The blood had attracted a smaller pack of wild dogs. Ordinarily, they would have scavenged for food, and picked at the remains left behind by their larger cousins; the Glacianne wolves. However, they could not resist the opportunity of such an easy meal. Freya was left alone with her injured companion, as the rest of the tribe had been herded like sheep. The dogs gritted their terrible teeth and snarled. The great wolf tried to stand, but it was too weak and fell flat to the floor. Freya stood and snarled back at them. She pulled a large blade from a holster on her hip and wielded a long spear in her other arm. She stabbed at the air in a devastating display. It did not deter the pack from pursuing their prey. Every time one took a step closer, Freya lashed at it to fend it off. More wild dogs had joined in the circle, until she was quickly surrounded. She tried to fend them off, but there were too many of them. One attacked her from behind and sunk its sharp serrated teeth into her calf. She stabbed it with her blade and kicked it free from her leg. Several of the other dogs jumped on their dead pack member and had begun to feast, while the others closed in on the injured pair. Freya had grown desperate. Facing her first and potentially final defeat, she gave one last swing of her spear and spun it in a circular motion to keep the dogs back. 'Ohmiya, where are you?' she shouted with the very last ounce of energy she could muster.

Just as the pack of wild dogs were about to pounce on their meal, a flash of blinding light illuminated before her. It startled the dogs and they backed away. 'You called for me?' said Ohmiya, and the light dispersed, leaving Ohmiya, Snowflake, Soria and Mr. Fuzzy stood in front of them.

Freya smiled a weak smile. 'Aren't you a sight for sore eyes.' She said and chuckled at the hopelessly perfect timing of her appearance. 'I would ask, how on earth you got here in such a heavenly manner? But, to be blunt, I am just glad you arrived when you did. I was about to become dinner. I would also ask, who is your friend? But that is a question, I think, that can wait until you tell us how we are to get out of this mess. Can I assume, as you appeared before me in such a grand way, that you were successful on your quest? And, that the white dragon knows of our troubles and told you how to resolve the problem at hand?'

Ohmiya held the hand of the exhausted Freya, and pulled her from the ground. She wrapped her arms around her tightly. 'I'm glad you are okay. I don't know what I would have done if I would have lost you too. And, my mother… is she?'

'She is fine, for now, but we must act quickly. Your friend, I'm sorry I do not know her name, can she help too?' asked Freya.

'Actually.' Said Ohmiya. 'She is the answer to all your questions. This is Soria from Athia, and her companion, Mr. Fuzzy.'

Freya raised an eyebrow and put her hands on her hips. 'Mr. Fuzzy? Isn't that the ridiculous name you were going to give Snowflake?' she said unimpressed.

Ohmiya clapped her hands and jumped excitedly. 'I knew I remembered that name from somewhere. I can't believe I had forgotten. Well, it suits him better anyway.'

Soria smiled. 'The difference being that my companion here was named ironically. Had I known what he was actually capable of, I might have thought of a more fitting name. And, it's nice to meet you by the way.' She said, and held out her hand.

Freya grabbed it and Soria squeezed her hand hard and shook it firmly. 'Likewise, and that is one hell of a grip you have their. I hope that you can fight too?' Freya said pleased. 'But, what can that thing do? I hope it's more than Snowflake here, because he's cute, sure, but he can't really do much.'

Ohmiya smiled smugly. 'Just wait. We will take it from here.' She said. 'You just stay here with your companion. This will all be over soon. This battle anyway.' She said.

'What do you mean, this battle?' Freya asked.

Soria stepped in. 'We'll explain later. Sit tight, we can take it from here. I think. Right Mr. Fuzzy?'

His fur fired up and the frozen floor beneath them melted away. Freya gawked with curiousness at the fuzzy little fireball, that burned with the power of a tiny star. Soria looked down on him, no longer in derision, but with admiration. She felt connected to her companion. She could feel his strength grow, and as he burned brighter, she too burned brighter. She lifted off the warm garments, that Ohmiya handed her, and handed them back to her as they were no longer needed. Her skin glowed with the same intensity as Mr. Fuzzy; everyone, and everything, stopped fighting. The very air around them became hot and humid. Solar flares flickered from his fur, and Soria's hair too started to burn a crimson red.

'Do you know your glowing?' Ohmiya asked from a safe distance, and continued to step backwards.

Soria looked at herself, startled as she saw her burning red skin. She looked at her companion, who then hopped onto her arm and licked her cheek. 'I think I'm starting to realise what the white dragon was talking about. We're stronger together.' She said and smiled at her companion, realising that their souls were now connected in an unbreakable bond. 'Let's do this.' She said.

The creatures of Glacia were still stood still and observing the blazing pair. Without fear, they hurled themselves into the fight and forced the creatures back. They clambered over each other in a mad panic, as the forest fire, that was Soria and Mr. Fuzzy, approached them at speed. The Glacianne hunters followed behind them, chanting and cheering sounds of victory. The war was won without further bloodshed on either side. Luckily, the fight had been stopped before any further loss of life, albeit some were terribly wounded. The bridge was burned by the blaze coming from the Athianne chieftainess and her companion, who, too, chanted cheers alongside the Glacianne.

The Glacianne tribe lifted Soria from her feet and hoisted her into the air. She crowd surfed the people, until she was at the feet of Nyssa. Ohmiya and Freya, too, stood by Nyssa, and they each curtsied Soria for her assistance. 'You have saved our people. We cannot hope to thank you enough for what you have done. We owe you a great debt.'

As Ohmiya, Nyssa and Freya lowered themselves to Soria, so too did the whole of the Glacianne tribe. She felt an enormous amount of pride as she stood within the crowd of bowing people. She had accomplished what she had set out to do, and become who she set out to be. With one selfless act, she had gained the respect of a people who were not her own. She had forged an unshakable bond with her companion, and forged a powerful new friendship. Humbled, and not expectant of the display of adoration, she lowered herself before the people. 'It was an honour to be able to assist you with your problem, and it was a privilege to help a friend in need.'

Nyssa gestured for Soria to raise herself from her curtsy. 'You will always have a friend here, for as long as you live. Your heroism here will be forever remembered. Stories will be told of this day. Of my daughter and Soria; the heroes who saved our people. If there is anything we can do for you in return, just say the word.'

Soria looked worried, about both her tribe and the favour she required of them. She did not wish to endanger a people she had just helped save, but she knew that her people would meet their end if she did not. 'I hate to ask this of you, and your people, just as they have evaded danger so narrowly. But, my people are in trouble. They are about to suffer the same fate your people nearly did if I do not return home to assist them. Ancient creatures, known as the lycunflame, presumed extinct, are about to attack my village. If I do not get back in time, I am afraid there will be no one to go back to. So, with a heavy heart, I ask that you help me and my tribe, the Athianne, fight off these monsters on the other side of the Sapphire Stream?'

The Glacianne tribe whispered loudly and conferred with one another. They wished to be told how it was possible for someone to have come across from the other side. No one had managed to dip a toe in the water, let alone make it across. How was it, that someone so young, had made it over alone they wondered? They continued to confer with each other, until Ohmiya commanded the silence of her tribe. She boomed her voice, as her father would have, over all the commotion. The crowd quietened momentarily and she gave a speech to the people. 'You will listen to your chieftainess while I speak. This brave warrior, and my very good friend, has saved our people from a truly terrible fate. Her people are about to be threatened by a very similar end. It is out of gratitude, for her unrequested, yet much needed assistance, that I am ordering we leave for Athia at once. Ready yourself for battle; this fight may have been won, but until our new allies on the other side of the Sapphire Stream are safe, the war is not yet over. Pick up your swords and spears, prepare yourself, as we leave at once.'

Nyssa placed her hand on her daughters shoulder. 'Your father would be very proud of the young woman you have become. Not one of us would have dared to do what you have done for the people. And although I share your desire to help Soria and her people, I am afraid that we have no way of travelling to Athia. We cannot pass the impassable stream. And even if we could, it would take days to reach them.'

Ohmiya placed her hand over her mother's and smiled. 'Don't worry about reaching Athia. You stay here with the people. They need you to help tend to the injured. We will take only the able bodied. Everyone else can stay behind. When we return, Glacia can be rebuilt.'

'I admire your courage daughter, but that does not explain how you intend on taking an army to Athia. It cannot be done.' Said Nyssa.

'It cannot be done on foot. But, luckily, we do not have to travel on foot. We can simply teleport there. Father was right, Snowflake was capable of more, and it was spending time with him and caring for him, that has allowed for him to grow into a companion fit for a leader. Only, Snowflake is one of a pair. He needed his counterpart, Mr. Fuzzy, to become who he was meant to be. Just as I needed Soria's help to become who I am meant to be. I could not have done any of this alone. And, now, she needs my help. So I won't let her down.'

Ohmiya boomed her voice again to the crowd of hunters, who had readied their weapons, yet were still unsure of how they were to reach their destination. 'Everyone, place your hand on the shoulder of the person next to you, until everyone is connected.' She waited for the crowd to do as she instructed, and they did so without hesitation.

Freya then placed her hand on the shoulder of Ohmiya. Ohmiya gently removed it. 'You cannot come, you are too weak to fight.' She said with concern.

Freya was outraged. Her companion howled at the notion of being left behind and stood firmly beside his keeper. His wounds looked severe, but just like Freya, he would not back away. She pulled tight the torn clothing that bound her and her companion's wounds. 'I have been preparing myself for a moment like this my whole life. I will not watch as our leader leaves to fight without me.' She said, then grabbed Ohmiya's shoulder tightly. 'This, little one, is an order I cannot allow you to make.'

Ohmiya frowned. 'Very well. If I cannot convince you to stay, then I would be honoured to have you fight by our side. But, if you come along and if you die, I will have no choice but to kill you. I cannot lose you too.' She said.

Freya laughed. 'You will not lose me today little one. And the honour will be all mine.'

Ohmiya gave one last order and told everyone to think of Athia. She knew the request was ludicrous, as no Glacianne had ever seen Athia, but it worked for Soria, when she had no recollection of a place she wished to be transported to. And, it was all they could do. The two young chieftainess' looked at each other for confirmation that the other was ready, nodded at each other, then spoke the words. 'The Athianne Village.'

Nyssa watched with bewilderment, as half of her tribes folk vanished in a flash of light. However, rather than ponder over the possibilities of how this had been possible, she turned her attention to the remaining Glacianne.

***

Argon had arrived back at the village; all was silent, yet he could sense danger was close by. He had returned in the hope that Soria had, too, returned. When he realised she hadn't, he decided that the best course of action was to take more of the tribe out to search for her at first light. They could cover more ground than he could alone.

His thoughts were split between the young leader's whereabouts and the injured fox he saw on his search for her. It had been centuries since anyone had killed another in Athia; human and animal alike. It was simply unheard of for one to eat the flesh of another living soul. This weighed heavy on his mind. He knew he could not hope to find Soria alone in the night, but he did not wish to leave her at the mercy of such a ferocious creature.

He checked the tents, to tend to those who had fallen ill in the heat. But all were sleeping when he returned; even Soria's parents were sleeping soundly. So he perched himself on a large rock on the outskirts of the village, and watched, awaiting the safe arrival of Aylen, Torch and his companion. He feared for her safety also, but was less concerned knowing she travelled with such a strong creature. He stared into the night sky on the lookout for his companion. The stars of Athia were hypnotic; it was not long before he succumbed to their effects and fell into a deep sleep.

Aylen laid back and rested upon the back of Torch. She stared at the stars as he galloped across the land on the way back to the village. With Soria AWOL, and her companion unresponsive, she had no choice but to sit back and wait. She looked relaxed, but she was far from it. If anyone had witnessed her threaten Soria, she would surely be accused of being the cause of her disappearance. The thought terrified her, as she did not wish to be banished from her home, nor worse, if the current chief found out. Although only seventeen, the punishment for treason would have been the same. Anyone from the age of twelve in Athia can be tried of a crime as an adult. Never in modern times had such a punishment been enacted. Never before had there been a need to carry out any of the laws, as everyone lived in relative piece. She did not wish to be the first.

The lycunflame were nearing the village. Their jaws widened and their mouths dripped with anticipation of Athianne for dinner. They stopped, only to snack on the unlucky animals that occupied the land at night. Rabbits made a tasty appetiser before the main course. Then, they continued to run like a stampede, co-ordinated yet chaotic, as they clambered amongst one another to be the first in the pack; to be the first one to take their pick of prey when they reached their destination. Although none had been to the village before, it was instinctive. It was coded in their DNA, and they knew exactly where to go for food.

Aylen sat up as Torch sped up. He galloped harder with no obvious reason for doing so. He howled into the night sky, and Argon's companion responded with a flash of flames. 'What is it boy?' she said. 'Please tell me what has you so riled.' He did not respond, he just panted.

She scouted ahead to look in the direction they were heading. 'Where heading back to the village? Is there something wrong? Are the rest of the tribe in trouble?' she asked.

Torch turned his head and looked at her sadly. She knew that something bad was happening, or was about to happen, she just did not know what that could be. Then, she saw it. The pack of lycunflame were dead ahead of them. Dust particles partially blocked her sight, so she shielded her eyes from the debris that was being flung into the air. They were a hundred metres away when Torch deviated to their right. He did not want them to be spotted.

Aylen stroked her companion on the tuft of his neck and whispered into his ear. 'Is that what we're chasing? Is that what has you so flustered?' she asked rhetorically.

She watched them from a distance as they passed them. Even from afar, she knew that they were nothing like she had ever seen before, she knew they were to be feared. Their blazing fangs shone bright in the blackness of the night. One turned to look at them, but turned away again. It was not interested in chasing down a meal, when an easier meal laid ahead. Torch ran swiftly ahead of them and made his way back to the village. He, too, was not interested in taking on the lycunflame head on. His target was the village, to warn the Athianne of what was due to arrive.

It was not long before Aylen and Torch returned home. They had beaten the beasts, but their time was short. Argon's companion squawked in the ear of her keeper until he fell from his place of rest. He stumbled to his feet, only to be knocked down again by Torch. It had knocked him over accidently in its attempt to stop. Aylen jumped from his back and grabbed him by the shirt. 'Unhand me child.' He said offended. 'What is it? Did you find her? Did you find Soria?'

Aylen let go of his shirt. 'No, I didn't. But...' She said frantically, then he stopped her from talking.

'Then there was no need to wake me so abruptly then was there? We shall form a search party in the morning, and search for her then. Go back to your tent and get some rest.' He said and had begun to yawn.

She grabbed him by his shirt again and pleaded for him to listen. 'You don't understand. We need to get everyone up. We need to get everyone away from here. Something is coming. Something terrible is coming.' She said. Then, she let go of his shirt again. Her hands were trembling, and her voice was shaking.

Argon began to ask, what it was that had caused her to be so afraid, but then stopped when he felt the ground rumble, and heard a low ruffling noise in the distance. 'What is it?' He said. 'What is coming?'

'I don't know. But if we don't get everyone out of here fast, I fear we will only live long enough to find out.' She said. 'You get everyone up and to safety. Me and Torch will stand and defend the village.'

Argon looked infuriated. 'You do not give the orders around here. I am in charge. You and Torch will be able to reach every tent faster than I can. You go get the people up and to safety. I will mount a defence.'

Aylen knew she should obey a direct order from someone in a more senior position than she. But, something compelled her to refuse. Something within her forced her to do what she knew was right. Torch was a formidable creature of incomprehensible power. She knew he was given to her for a reason. She knew deep down, that he was the only creature in the village that could stand up to what was coming. Argon was strong, and his companion was impressive, but she had seen what was heading their way. She knew that her and Torch would be the only ones who could keep them at bay until everyone was safely away. It was not a decision to refuse

Argon, it was instinctive. 'No!' she ordered. 'Respectfully, I will not be running away with everyone else, as I fear you will not last longer than a few minutes against what is coming, and will inevitably seal all our fates. You will round everyone up and lead them away from the village, towards the Sapphire Stream. Torch and I will stand guard and make sure everyone has gotten to safety. Then, if we make it, we will catch up to you later. There is no time to deliberate the matter any further. I will grant you the time you need.' She said. And, before he had time to respond, Torch ignited with a white-hot flame. Aylen, too, blazed with the same fire of her companion, and they were gone before Argon could move his lips to speak.

'Well I'll be damned.' He said with a chuckle. 'I would've never thought she'd be the one giving orders one day.' He murmured under his breath. His companion landed on his shoulder, screeched in his ear, and he began to head towards the chief's tent.

He could not be roused. The heat had sent him into a state of hibernation. He tried the rest of the village, but the really young and old alike could not be awoken. Only a handful of Athianne and their companions gathered. Most of which were teenagers and those in their early twenties. They were confused as to why they had been gathered at such an ungodly hour. Argon, unsure himself what was heading their way, could only tell them what he knew. 'There is something heading this way, something terrible. Retreat was the plan, but there are too many people still asleep. The heat has caused their sickness to worsen. We cannot hope to get them away from here in time. So, we must ready ourselves.'

'Ready ourselves for what Argon?' asked a frightened fourteen-year-old.

'I do not know exactly. I saw something out in the plains today. It had me worried, so I called for my companion to fetch Aylen and Torch back to the village. But, when she returned, she confirmed my fears. *"Something terrible is coming,"* she said. She is bravely heading towards what is coming, to grant us the time we need to leave. I do not believe, however, that we will be able to leave before whatever is coming arrives. I fear it is already upon us. So you must choose a weapon, or anything that could be reasonably used as a weapon. Then we must head east of the village. It is there that we will make our stand. We must help Aylen to protect the village.

The Athianne had begun to chatter amongst themselves in an agitated state. They had not taken his words as seriously as they should have, because no Athianne had ever known war. No Athianne had ever had a threat placed upon them before. Their response was, not to quickly assemble themselves for battle, but to confer with one another of the best course of action.

Argon was not amused with their lack of urgency. 'Now!' he boomed.

The young Athianne began to scramble and knocked into one another as they tried to gather their chosen weapons. They returned momentarily with broomsticks, pitchforks, spades for digging up roots, and a handful of blunt knifes that were used to cut berries from branches. Like a handful of well-equipped farmers, they were ready and waited for Argons next order. He looked out over his troops with worry, took a deep breath and composed himself. 'I do not know what waits for us out there. I do not know what we are about to face. But what I do know, is you should be scared. I do know that whatever is coming, is not like anything we have ever seen before. No one here, not even I, have ever had to fight. It is simply unheard of in Athia. But, we are a strong people, we are a hard people, and we will not be intimidated by anyone, or anything. This may be the first time we have had to defend ourselves, but it may not be the last. I believe, though, that learning on the job and being thrown in at the deep end is still the best way to learn.' He said sternly, then gestured for all to follow him.

The Athianne marched east, and headed towards the outskirts of Athia, ready to fight against an unknown threat.

Aylen waited patiently, like the commander-in-chief of an army of one. She and Torch were all that stood between the village and a cloud of dust that hurtled at speed towards them. It got closer, and closer, until the dust cloud stopped. It had begun to settle momentarily. Burning through the debris was the lycunflames' fangs; a hundred flaming knives faced her. Their large, slanted, blood red eyes narrowed and the wolves barked ferociously like wild dogs. Torch barked back at them and scratched at the floor with his front paws, like a bull ready to charge.

The lycunflame were not stopped for long. Torch may have stood slightly taller; however, he was but one wolf. The hoard had numbers on their side and they were not going to be intimidated by a solitary creature. So, they set out on a rampage. Aylen tugged at Torch's fur like a rider at a horse's rains and ordered him to stand his ground. He bounced on his front paws, like a horse awaiting release from its box in a race. 'Hold it there, wait a little longer.' She said. Then, she ordered him to charge. He burst from the spot like a firework and headed dead centre of the crowd. They were in striking distance of one another and were about to attack. But, they were stopped. A wall of fire emerged before them, blocked the lycunflame from crossing and forced Aylen and Torch to pull back.

A voice called her from behind. 'You didn't really think that I was going to leave you to fight alone did you?' said Argon. His phoenix had created a wall of fire between them and the hoard of lycunflame. 'That will not hold them for long. But it should bide us some time. I can't believe you intended on fighting them monsters on your own; are you out of your mind?'

'It was all I could think to do.' She replied. 'How else were we to get everyone to safety?'

'That is where your age deceives you little one. You have grown brave, but you lack the wisdom that comes with age.' Argon continued. 'You are strong, there is no doubt of that; maybe you are the strongest of all of us. But we are stronger together. Athianne do not leave other Athianne behind.'

Aylen smiled in relief. 'I had hoped that would be the case. Bravery, it seems, is not all it's cracked up to be. And, I have come to learn, it is simply well masked fear.' She said.

Argon turned to face his people, who, although looked immensely strong, with faces like angry bulls, were terrified of what lay beyond the blaze. Brushes and pitchforks trembled in their palms, as they awaited the flames to fall and release what was on the opposite side; the lycunflame.

The wolves did not wait for the flames to cease, as it is said, that they were born from the lava pits of the mountains, when the mountains were once volcanic. Their blood red, hungry eyes, peered through the wall of fire, then they walked through as though it wasn't even there. Everyone gasped as they entered the light and every vicious feature became visible.

'It can't be.' Argon said. 'They don't exist, they aren't real. Just a story, a silly children's story is what they are.'

'Well they look pretty damn real to me.' Said Aylen. 'I know that the heat can play tricks on the mind, cause us to hallucinate; maybe. Yet, I doubt we are all sharing the same hallucination.'

The Athianne, most of which were only in their mid-teens, were scrambling in panic. Those at the front were pushing to the back, and those at the back, were pushing one another to the front. Their companions were being crushed under the chaos. No one wished to fight, no one wished to die.

Aylen watched this. She knew she had to stand up and say something. Something inside her forced itself out and she felt compelled to say something. 'Stop!' she continued. 'You are only riling them up! They can smell your fear, and it is driving them forward. Pull yourselves together. I want everyone in a line. No one at the front, and no one at the back. We are equal and we will fight as equals. All in one line. We are Athianne, and we must act as we are perceived to be. We are a hard people. Everyone band together, no gaps, and stop them from getting to the village.' She ordered.

The Athianne looked up to Aylen, who straddled the great wolf, Torch. She spoke in a commanding tone and defused the tension instantly with her words. Even Argon, who was ill at ease with taking orders from anyone but the chief, seconded her cry for order. The Athianne, although scared, did as they were asked. One row of people chained themselves together in a long line that blocked the way. The lycunflame did not falter, and continued to creep closer.

Argon grabbed a sweeping brush from someone who held two, snapped the end off against the ground, and began to bash the dull end against the floor in a repetitive beat. The rest of the Athianne had begun to do the same and the noise echoed across the plains and down through the village. Aylen was thrown a pitchfork with the curved ends straitened, until it looked more like a pronged spear, and she lunged it threateningly into the air. The lycunflame stopped for a moment in confusion, then without warning, they began to rampage.

***

Soria, along with Ohmiya and the Glacianne hunters, had arrived in a burst of light on the west side of the village. The air had boiled every drop of moisture from the surface. The ground was broken and covered in cracks. Freya fell to the floor and cried out in pain, so too did the rest of the Glacianne. The heat was too intense. Even Soria struggled to catch her breath. Soria watched in horror as the tribe that had offered her aid, were being killed by the land they had come to save.

Ohmiya had fallen at her feet and was screaming in agony. 'Help us!' she called out to her friend. 'Help us, Soria!'

'I don't know what to do!' she panicked, then looked around for help. She could see no one, she could hear no one. All her tribe had seemingly succumb to the searing heat of Athia. She picked up Mr. Fuzzy. 'Do something!' she cried. 'Do something please!'

Her companion did not do anything, as he could not do anything. So she placed him on the ground and cried out for anyone to help, for anything to help. No one answered her call. She fell to her knees and began to cry. *What have I done?* She thought, *What have I done? This is all my fault.* Her tears evaporated into the air as she continued to cry. 'What do I do now?' she said aloud through her sobbing. 'Tell me, what I am supposed to do now?' she looked up and roared into the sky.

As she looked up, something peculiar happened, something peculiar fell from the sky and landed on the end of her nose; it was a snowflake. The snowflake did not melt, it remained sparkling. Another then fell, and landed on her finger. Then, another one touched the back of her neck, and she felt a mild chill run down her spine. The air then started to cool gradually, and snow had begun to fall all around them. It was the most bizarre of things; snow in Athia. Not just any snow, but snow that was settling. Soria saw mist leave her lips as she let out of warm breath, and felt the cold air scratch her throat as she breathed back in. From impossibly hot, to impossibly cold within a matter of minutes.

The Glacianne's rose from the floor like the dead rising and laughed. They laughed at the oddity of such an event. All looked up as large flakes of snow fell like falling leaves in the autumn. 'How is this possible?' said Soria, and she looked around for an answer.

'I guess the white dragon was right about both our companions.' Said Ohmiya, and Soria turned to face her. There, with an electric blue glow, stood Ohmiya and Snowflake. They were emitting an arctic breeze and sparkling like the freshly forming snow. 'I guess that Snowflake has more to show us, too.'

Their glow had then begun to dim, but the air remained cool. Once the Glacianne had finished wondering what had happened, they formed a crowd around the young chieftainess. 'Are we here? Did we make it to Athia?' asked Freya.

Ohmiya, unsure also if they had arrived, looked inquisitively at Soria. 'We're here.' She replied, then looked at the village. Untouched, unaltered and eerily quiet. Not even the odd person pottering around. The Glacianne followed her into the village, and, so too did the cool air. Wherever Snowflake and Ohmiya went, the cool breeze and a flurry of snow followed.

Soria ran to her parents tent, to check they were still safe, to check that nothing had yet happened. Ohmiya ordered her tribe to check the other tents and watch out for wolves. Then, she met up with Soria at her home.

'Thank goodness they're safe.' Soria sighed with relief. 'We must have gotten here on time.' She said.

Freya walked in behind them. 'I wouldn't be too sure of that.' She put her head down. 'The other tents are mostly empty. All the others are filled with elderly people and children. It's as though half of your people have vanished. Where would they be? Would they be anywhere else but here?' she asked hopefully.

Soria shook her head. 'No, they would all be here, unless…
Unless something has happened to them.' She said.

Ohmiya placed her hands on Soria's shoulders for reassurance.
'Don't say that. You don't know anything has happened to them yet.
There is no sign of a struggle. There is nothing here to suggest that
anyone is hurt. Right Freya?' Ohmiya looked to her for words of
comfort.

Freya, who knew that most hunting animals carried their prey
away to eat, had assessed the area. *No claw marks on the tents, no
fresh tracks on the ground, no fresh blood and no smell of death,*
she pondered for an awkward length of time, before she confirmed
Ohmiya's assessment of the situation. 'Yes. I can honestly say, that I
don't believe anything bad has happened here yet. But, if you are
right, and your tribe is in danger, then they are still in danger, which
means we are in danger at present. We can no longer linger around
the tents in such a disorderly fashion, as we will be picked off one by
one, like the weak links in a herd. Where would these creatures be
coming from, so we can ready ourselves for their arrival, and catch
them off guard?' asked Freya.

Soria, thankful that they were still in time to prevent any harm
coming to her tribe, pointed east. 'They would be coming from the
east, from where the cave is, where the red dragon slumbers. We
should head that way if we are to intercept them.'

251

The three were leaving the tent when Ceyhan met them at the opening. 'Come quick.' She said. 'Come quick.' She repeated.

'What is it?' asked Soria.

'There is a noise coming from the east side of the village. It sounds like a low booming noise. It sounds like the beating of drums in the distance.' She said.

That's odd. Thought Soria, as there was no event taking place that she was aware of. And in the case of any event, she had never known of drums being used. 'That can't be a good sign.' She said. 'It may be someone signalling for help.' She cried and headed in that direction.

She ran as fast as her legs would carry her and left the Glacianne, who she had brought to aid her, in a mad dash to find out who was making the noise. Ohmiya and Freya assembled the rest of the Glacianne and they headed east after her.

'You ready for this?' Ohmiya asked Freya.

Freya smiled with delight. 'This is what I was born for. I have been waiting for a moment like this my whole life.' She said.

'It's a rather odd thing to look forward to isn't it?' Ohmiya said.

'I was born a warrior in a place with no war to fight. War is not something I have been looking forward to, but something I have craved. It may sound odd to you, but it makes all the sense in the world to me. I hope, little chieftainess, you are ready for what you are walking in to.' She replied.

'I am ready to fight for my friend. This much I know. She helped save my people, and did so without a second thought. I owe her nothing less than the same in return.' Ohmiya said. Then, with Freya by her side, she led the Glacianne tribe east of the Athianne village.

The Athianne charged at the lycunflame, and were led into battle by Aylen and Torch. The ravenous wolves barged at each other to get to the front and pushed one another aside. The largest of the hoard was heading towards Torch, accompanied by two others. The smaller two gnashed and gnawed at his front paws and held him down. The largest one sunk its fangs deeply into the side of his neck and thrashed around trying to bring him down for the kill. Aylen thrust her improvised spear into the smaller lycunflame, and they let go with a whimper. Torch, then rose again to his feet and lifted the largest of the wolves, who was still attached to his neck, and began to burn with a white hot flame. The wolf would not let go of Torch willingly, and maintained its grip. Torch would not be brought down again, though. The large monster that dangled from his neck was thrashing around like a fish caught on a line. Torch tilted his neck, just enough to reveal an opening, and Aylen trust the spear into its side with ferocity. It let go instantly and fell to the floor with a thud. It tried to run away. But, Torch was rearing and readying itself to stomp. Then, it came down on the monster with all its weight and trampled it into the ground.

Argon ran straight into the centre of the hoard, slid under one of the lycunflame, then thrust his sharpened broom handle into the torso of the wolf. Its great weight fell on him, and he struggled to lift it off. Another wolf saw him struggle, and was heading toward him. It moved slowly and licked it's lips as it approached him, watching him try to squirm free. Another lycunflame had also noticed the easy meal that lay under one of their dead. It tackled the other wolf to the ground, and they had begun fighting amongst themselves, over who would be the first to taste his flesh. Argon, although fascinated by their brawl, was not prepared to wait and to see who was to be the victor. He tried and tried to pull himself free, but was unable.

One of the wolves had won their right to draw first blood, and the other stood down and pulled away. Argon watched as it smiled a hideous smile and its fangs began to flame. He had witnessed first-hand the work of the jaws that approached him, and did not want to end up like the fox. He tried desperately to pull the weapon from under the monster he slayed. But, he could not move his arm; it was too heavy. He could taste the wolf's last victim on the breath of the beast. It was within inches of his face. Then, a mighty caw called from the sky. Argon's companion fell from the sky like a shooting star and drove it's beak into the skull of the wolf. It hit the ground dead. The other wolf saw its chance and jumped into the air with its mouth gaping wide. Argon shielded his face with his free arm and awaited his fate. Nothing happened, though. He lifted his arm and revealed the lycunflame limp in the air, held tightly in the jaws of Torch. Torch threw it through the air and it sailed into another lycunflame. He then lifted the dead wolf on top of Argon into the air, freeing him from his fleshy prison and pulled him to his feet.

'Well that's twice you saved my life today. And, to think that you were once that timid little thing, that couldn't even make it down the mountain all those years ago.' He said.

'Well, I guess I was just a late bloomer.' Said Aylen with a smirk, who sat strongly upon Torch's back. 'But, now is no time for thanks. We are still massively outnumbered and struggling to hold them all back. It's only a matter of time before they break through our ranks and head towards the village. We need a miracle to get us through this.' She said.

The Athianne fought bravely against the lycunflame; an enemy that outnumbered them greatly and outmatched them in every way. It took two or three people to take down a wolf, and the wolves had two or three in their pack for every one Athianne that stood against them. Aylen watched as her tribe tired from fighting. The injured fell back, and those who were able, defended the wounded. Their companions were not fit for battle, but they fought back courageously to defend their keepers.

Baasim, a young Athianne boy, no older than thirteen, was knocked from his feet. Leaning over him was the dripping wet tongue of a lycunflame. It snapped back its jaws and snatched away his stick. He cried out for help, but Aylen was too far away. She ordered Torch to get to him, so he strode at speed across the battlefield. They watched in slow motion, as the wolf went to devour Baasim in one bite. Then, it stopped. Soria picked up the stick that had been tossed aside, skewered it into the side of the beast, and pushed it off the boy.

Aylen pulled up beside her. 'You're alive!' she said.

'You sound relieved.' Soria said sarcastically.

'I am relieved and I am sorry. We looked everywhere for you. We feared the worst. I never meant what I said before. I didn't mean it. I am truly glad you're safe.' Aylen replied.

Soria smiled and looked admiringly at Aylen. 'Thanks. But, you did mean what you said. And, you were right. I deserved what was said to me, needed for someone to stand up to me, even. I was a horrible person, and it needed someone like you to tell me straight. Although, admittedly, I would never have expected it to be you to say something to me. Nevertheless, we can make up later anyway. Now, I think, you could do with some help getting rid of these infernal creatures.' Said Soria.

Aylen smiled back. 'That we do, but I'm afraid that we are in need of more than one person to help us win this fight. Although I am glad you are back, you may have returned only to share our fate. We need an army to fight these creatures off.' She said.

Soria laughed and gestured behind her. 'An army you say. Well I guess that we are in luck, as it just so happens, an army is what I have brought back with me.' Said Soria.

A cool breeze swept over the battlefield, as Ohmiya and Snowflake appeared, followed closely by Freya, her wolf, and over a hundred heavily armed Glacianne hunters; each accompanied by their companions.

The bitter breeze bit into the wolves' and they began to back off a little. Never before had the Athianne prayed for a cooler climate, but the drop in temperature was welcomed by the heat exhausted people.

The Athianne cheered upon the arrival of their unknown allies. The Glacianne stormed into the fight without any need for invitation. Freya was the first to attack and happily plunged her knife into the hide of a lycunflame. She tore through the hoard of beasts, forgetting about her injury and the pain it caused her. Her face beamed with unnerving delight, as she took them on one after the other. Her companion, also forgetting his pain, pinned them down in his jaws, as Freya went in for the final blow.

The Glacianne followed her into the fight and the lycunflames' numbers had quickly begun to dwindle. Soria, Ohmiya and their companions accompanied Aylen and Torch. Aylen watched in surprise as the two balls of fur showed off their immense powers. Mr. Fuzzy seared with the strength of a tiny star and scorched all who came in too close. Snowflake, an equally bizarre little being, impaled the creatures with crystal pines that shot from his fur. Those that went in to bite him, were frozen solid.

The air turned colder with every passing moment. The lycunflames' fangs were no longer ablaze, and they had lost the advantage of their numbers. The few that remained became confused in the cold, and some had already fled. As the people of both tribes marched forward, the lycunflame coward back. Until, all that remained were a few injured stragglers. They swiftly succumbed to the cold and fell soon after.

The Athianne roared with delight as the last of the lycunflame fell, and their homes and their people were once again safe. Soria sighed with relief and fell to the floor with fatigue from her long journey. So, too, did Ohmiya and they were carried back to the village by the people.

Three days had passed, when the two young chieftainess finally awoke from their sleep. Stood over them were familiar faces. Side by side, were Soria's father, mother and Freya. 'Thank goodness you are okay. You both had us worried for a while. We thought that you would never wake up.'

They rose gradually from their beds and sat up awkwardly, still in pain from the multiple injuries they had sustained. They stared at one another and shared a look of dissatisfaction. Relieved as they were, thankful as they were that the ordeal was over, they couldn't help but be saddened at the fact that their time together had come to an end. It was hard for them to imagine returning to their respective tribes, and fulfilling a destiny that no longer lined with their desire. Neither of the girls wished to lead anymore; they only wished to lead their own future. Without saying a single word, and with only a single look, they knew what they had to do. As though they also shared a profound connection, like that of their companions. It could not be explained, it was just instinctive. This adventure, the one that they started alone, then were drawn to one another by fate, had come to an end. But their adventures together, they knew, had only just begun.

Epilogue

A few months had passed since the young chieftainess' had declined the titles they were born to uphold. A few things had changed on both sides of the Sapphire Stream, which now returned to a state of stability.

The white dragon recovered and upheld his promise to restore the Glacianne City back to its former glory. He flattened the remaining scales which stood precariously, thus laying the foundation for a newer, larger, stronger city. Aylen, for her heroism and notable strength, was offered the title of chieftainess of Glacia. Her and Torch happily accepted and they returned home with her new tribe.

Freya stayed behind. The lycunflame were just the first of many potential dangers. The world that was once sealed off from Athia had now been revealed, so she stayed to assist in training the tribe in the art of war, so that they could defend themselves against future threats. However, it was something that she once considered an affliction that also drew her to stay. It was a feeling that she had repelled with detest with great success, until she met Argon. He, too, felt the same way, and from the day they crossed paths, they did not stray from one another. It was a fitting union, as Soria asked that they take her place, and lead the Athianne as chief and chieftainess of the tribe. A great wall was built, like that of Glacia, and the bond between tribes was now as strong as the walls that guarded them.

As for our heroes, they stayed for a while and watched as both their people flourished. The red dragon was awoken by his brother, the white dragon, and he burned away the ice that blocked the path across the Sapphire Stream, so that both sides were then accessible. But, after a while, their thirst for adventure grew too great for them to contain. The high rocky surface that was once unclimbable, and impassable, had cracked from the quakes and everything that had come to pass. So, one night, without so much as a goodbye, Soria, Mr. Fuzzy, Ohmiya and Snowflake, wandered out into the unknown world...

Gareth Jackson